# UNBREAK MY HEART

Despite her broken heart, artist Roberta Armstrong has put everything into rebuilding her business and her life. Whilst her friend Lee wants to take their friendship further, she is determined not to let anyone become close to her again. Then Charles arrives . . . Slowly her heart begins to mend, and she truly feels she can put her tragic past behind her. But is Charles hiding something? And will Bobbie ever be able to learn to trust again?

*Books by Beth James*
*in the Linford Romance Library:*

IT STARTED WITH A KISS

013000847X

BETH JAMES

# UNBREAK MY HEART

*Complete and Unabridged*

LINFORD
*Leicester*

First published in Great Britain in 2006

First Linford Edition
published 2008

British Library CIP Data

James, Beth
  Unbreak my heart.—Large print ed.—
  Linford romance library
  1. Love stories
  2. Large type books
  I. Title
  823.9′2 [F]

  ISBN 978–1–84782–071–6

Published by
F. A. Thorpe (Publishing)
Anstey, Leicestershire

Set by Words & Graphics Ltd.
Anstey, Leicestershire
Printed and bound in Great Britain by
T. J. International Ltd., Padstow, Cornwall

This book is printed on acid-free paper

# 1

'Oh no, not again. When will this guy get the message?' Impatiently Roberta tossed the unopened letter on to the pile waiting to be shredded.

Mel looked up from the envelope she was opening. 'What's up, Bobbie?' she queried. 'You haven't even read it yet.'

'Don't need to,' replied Bobbie tucking a strand of her thick pale brown hair behind her ear. 'It's that Spike friend of John's. Wants to see me. Wants to talk old times. He's a pain in the neck. Even had the nerve to contact my mum at Christmas — so what happens? I get a card and a letter from him and now, another letter.'

From over the top of the electricity bill, Mel regarded the angry face of her friend. 'Shouldn't you maybe read it before chucking it away?' she suggested tentatively.

'What for? I know it's from him. Recognise the writing, recognise the postmark. How many people do I know in Windermere?'

'Aren't you even mildly curious?'

Roberta shrugged and turned away. She had a blanked-off feeling. She'd experienced the same sensation over and over again during the last eighteen months. It happened every time she was forced to think about John.

John with his wide grin, his freckles, his way of making even the smallest incident seem like fun. John, with his easy kisses, his easy promises, and his inability to keep them.

She looked across at Mel, her best friend, her saviour. 'I've told you before. That part of my life is over. Finished. I've tried writing to that effect but no, this guy is just too dumb to realise it. I had one of these two weeks ago, ignored that one too. It's the only way.'

So saying, Bobbie picked up the blue envelope with its large, loopy, distinctive handwriting and pushed it through the shredder. Then she turned and smiled ruefully at her friend. 'Wish I could do that with the rest of these,' she said motioning towards a stack of bills.

Mel pulled a face. 'I know what you mean, but let's look on the bright side. You know I told you we had a room cancelled yesterday, for this week? Well, we've got two more bookings from the Internet for next month and one I've just opened in this morning's post for a double weeks' booking in July. That means that apart from one empty room this week, we're almost fully booked until the end of August, so it's not all bad news.'

The two girls exchanged glances. It had been a risk, investing everything they had into what once had been an ordinary, rather run-down, bed and breakfast business.

Then somehow keeping it running, while they had a new wing added and opened up the main part of the barn to become a large art studio.

In this, their first complete year, they

were relying on having steady bookings from Easter to October to keep themselves solvent, but hadn't really expected to be so popular that there were no vacancies at all.

'Shame the cancellation was at such short notice. Too late to ring the waiting list, I suppose?' asked Bobbie.

Shaking her dark curls, Mel gave an exasperated sigh. 'Lighten up Bobbie, will you? It's great. We're doing really well. One cancellation is not the end of the world.'

Once the sorting out of the post was finished, Bobbie left Mel to check the week's menus, and made her way to the studio part of Painter's Barn in order to organise the art materials that the next influx of paying guests, due to arrive that afternoon, would require.

She pushed open the heavy oak door and couldn't help the small shiver of pride that spiralled through her.

Mel was right; she should lighten up, be more aware of their achievements, stop worrying about the future and just regard the whole thing as a wonderful adventure.

The barn was light and airy, with a high ceiling and exposed rafters. One end of it was completely given over to studio space where Bobbie would give demonstrations then supervise her pupils' work. Although supervise was the wrong word really, because she believed very strongly in allowing her students to develop at their own pace and only gently nudged them in the right direction when she deemed it absolutely necessary.

Bobbie loved her work. One of the studio's walls was completely covered with her acrylic canvasses, and another with framed samples of her watercolours. They were all for sale, but sadly she couldn't sell enough to support herself. And anyway, much as she loved painting and drawing, she found encouraging other people in their new found talents even more rewarding.

The south end of Painter's Barn housed a dining-room and kitchen. This end was Mel's domain. It was here that she cooked and presented the most mouth-watering meals for the guests. The wing to the west of this was where the office and Bobbie's tiny flat were positioned.

The eastern wing of the barn contained six double bedrooms with ensuites. This was where the PGs, the paying guests, stayed.

The barn was quite isolated, a fact not really noticeable in the painting season when Bobbie knew there were always people around, even on changeover days when help from the village made their presence felt, cleaning and changing beds. But next winter, Bobbie knew it would be very different.

Last winter had been OK because Mel had been living in the other half-finished wing, and builders, plumbers and electricians had been in an out of the place. But in February Mel had married Tom and moved one and a half miles away to Sway, and even though

Bobbie had some adult learning classes lined up with the council, she dreaded feeling cold and lonely in the huge barn for most of next winter's dark winter months.

However, it was still only late March so she wasn't going to think of next winter yet, it was miles away. She had to check her supplies of tubes of watercolours, packs of paper and brushes ready for the new arrivals.

The partnership between Roberta and Mel worked well. Mel took care of most of the domestic organisation, while Bobbie concentrated on running the art classes. The students' rooms consisted of two single rooms, but each of the other six rooms offered two single beds with en-suite. The courses were proving popular and the setting of the New Forest perfect.

Bobbie was able to arrange field trips to nearby Christchurch with its cathedral and interesting boatyard area and also to Bournemouth and Lymington, not to mention the picturesque scenery and wildlife that existed right on the doorstep.

Not for the first time Bobbie told herself how very lucky she was. So why then did she heave a sigh as she noted she was out of cobalt blue and sap green yet again, even though she repeatedly encouraged her students to mix their own greens and to try a blue other than cobalt for a change? It was hardly a hardship to have to take a trip to the wholesalers and pick up more paint, now was it?

Bobbie compiled her list. She visited the wholesaler on a monthly basis. Many of her more experienced students brought their own materials, merely adding to them when they ran out of something or maybe a new brush caught their eye. Others, usually the beginners, either had the wrong things or more often, nothing at all. Consequently Bobbie was never sure exactly what her requirements would be month on month.

She made her way out of the studio

and to the office in order to e-mail her order through to the wholesaler then, on a sudden whim, decided to make a personal visit and, browsed around the big *shed* as she called the stationer's warehouse she used.

The childhood fascination of pens, paint and paper had never left her. In her student days, Bobbie had spent far more time examining, obtaining, and rejecting materials, than she ever spent wondering what to wear. To her a visit to a stationer's was like a trip to an Aladdin's cave, there was a certain smell, a certain invitation about the shelves of brightly-coloured tubes of paint, pots of pencils and stacks of paper, she regarded as magical.

So after a shouted explanation to Mel and with an unfamiliar lightness of heart, Bobbie climbed into her car, drove cautiously down the rather uneven gravel driveway towards the main road. You're a sad case, she told herself. Getting excited about a visit to the wholesalers.

'Hi, long time no see!'

Bobbie looked up from the new pastel paper she was examining. 'Morning, Lee.'

'Haven't seen you for ages. Where've you been hiding?'

'Oh, busy. You know how it is.' Bobbie passed her list across to the large young man facing her.

'Thanks.' His fingers brushed hers in a way she knew was not entirely accidental. She quickly put her hand in the pocket of her denim jacket and adopted a serious expression. Lee's eyes smiled across at her. 'Got some new stock in,' he said. 'I was going to give you a bell anyway. Some good-sized canvasses. Ideal for acrylics — don't cost the earth either.'

'Hmm. OK, I'll look. I'm not buying any yet though. No more acrylics until the courses finish. The courses are strictly watercolour and once I start using acrylics I get very heavy handed

10

with the watercolour and ladylike watercolours — which is what most of my students want to produce — go out the window.'

Lee led the way into the back of the warehouse which was piled up with computer equipment, office materials and eventually the canvasses.

Bobbie's eyes opened wide. 'Wow, these would be great for some of my abstract work.'

Lee looked pleased with himself. 'Knew you'd like them,' he said in a satisfied voice. 'Shouldn't work too wet though with the really big ones. They've got stretchers of course, but I wouldn't like to say how effective they'd be on the larger sizes.'

Bobbie turned towards him. 'Thanks Lee,' she said. 'I can't take them off your hands right now, no space, but I will try some — I promise. It was very good of you to think of me.'

'Do it all the time . . . Think of you that is.'

Oh dear. Bobbie turned away. 'I bet

you say that to all the girls,' she threw at him over her shoulder.

'As it happens — no. How about a trip to London — do the art galleries?'

Swallowing, Bobbie kept walking forward between the stacks of office equipment. She kept her tone light. 'Maybe, at the end of the season I'll find time. But right now, well, I'm pretty busy. Thanks though, nice of you to ask.'

'Well, that's me — Mr Nice Guy. Doesn't get me far though, does it?'

Bobby laughed. 'Come on, Lee. We're mates. Don't go all sorry for yourself on me.'

A ready smile spread across Lee's good-looking features and he ran a hand over his closely-cropped fair hair. 'OK let's see if your order's ready for you. I'll catch up with you in the pub one of these days when you get a free evening.'

A wave of relief washed over Bobbie. It looked as though Lee was ready to follow her lead of keeping things light this time. There had been other times when there had been signs that he wanted to change the bantering relationship, they'd had ever since their student days, into something more serious. Signs that so far, Bobbie had been able to gently rebuff but she dreaded his becoming more persistent.

Lee had always been a stalwart companion, even through those awful weeks eighteen months ago when her whole world had collapsed and she'd shut herself off from everyone.

Yes, Lee along with Mel and her husband Tom, had proved himself a good friend, which was why Bobbie found it so difficult to make him understand that a friend was all she ever wanted him to be.

Just then, Lee was called to the telephone and a relieved Bobbie checked off her order with the help of an assistant then, with some difficulty, carried her new purchases to her car. Aware that she'd spent longer than she'd intended browsing in The Shed, she glanced at her watch and gave an involuntary start. Although the guests shouldn't arrive until after lunch, there was still a lot to do and she couldn't leave Mel to cope alone.

Just as she started the engine Lee's grinning face appeared at the windscreen. 'You weren't going to sneak off without saying goodbye were you?'

Bobbie wound down the window. 'Sorry Lee, I've just realised how late it is. Got to get a wiggle on — it's change over day.'

But Lee carried on leaning on the car door. 'What's your rush? Expecting someone special? Some dark-haired stranger perhaps, to sweep you off your feet? If you are, perhaps I should warn him, being swept off your feet is not something you'd take kindly to.'

Bobbie gave a laugh that was a little more forced than she intended. 'You're so right. Glad you got the message. Thanks for your help, Lee. Maybe I'll catch you later.' So saying, she raised her hand in a comradely wave and released the handbrake.

Once underway, the smile left her face. Why couldn't Lee leave her alone Couldn't he see she was quite happy as she was? She didn't need, or want any handsome stranger, dark or otherwise, sweeping her off her feet. The last time that had happened it had ended in disaster. No, worse than disaster — tragedy. A repeat performance was the last thing on her agenda.

No, she was happy enough as she was. She had a demanding job that she loved and family further down in Hampshire that she was close to. She had friends living nearby, including Lee, that she'd known most of her life, so why did everyone seem to assume that because she'd had no boyfriend for eighteen months, she was unhappy and needed taking out of her herself?

Bobbie frowned a little. When she phoned home her mother would gently probe as to whether she was getting out more these days. Bobbie knew that this was her mother's shorthand for — was there any possibility of romance with a capital R on the horizon? It didn't seem to matter how many times Bobbie insisted that, thank you very much, romance was not what she was looking for. She'd tried that, didn't want to try it again.

After all what did romance do to you? It turned you into an idiot. It made you believe in perfection personified. Made you think that one person and only one, held the key to your happiness. Lulled you into a false sense of security. Then, when you were feeling happier than you'd ever thought possible this side of heaven — then what happened?

You found out, that your perfect person was capable of horrendous deceit, that they broke promises. That romance was make believe. That love was nothing but an illusion.

Bobbie gripped the steering wheel very hard. She was not going to cry, she'd done with crying a long time ago.

John was no longer around. John

broke promises. John was dead.

No, romance was out. Friendship was good. Bobbie could handle friendship. Mel and Tom; trusted friends from years ago like — Lee, for instance. Yes, she trusted Lee, despite not feeling in the least romantic towards him, she knew he'd never let her down. And she was happy enough now, wasn't she? Well, not ecstatic of course, but she didn't want ecstasy did she? She wanted calm, peace, tranquillity.

Nodding to herself as though she'd just won an important argument, Bobbie turned the car up the gravel driveway and parked next to a rather snazzy Porsche. Her eyebrows shot up, as mentally, Bobbie ticked off the students she was expecting this week. The Porsche was hardly the transport of the vicar and his wife, several members of an art club for retired folk from Kent, or the two spinster history teachers from East Hanningfield that they were expecting.

She gave a grin and retrieved the

newly-purchased materials from the boot. See, life was full of surprises. Who said her life was dull?

Gripping her keys between her teeth, her arms full of the new reams of paper and tubes of paint, not to mention her shoulder bag, Bobbie pushed open the barn door with the only other part of her anatomy that was left — her bottom.

'Oh dear, terribly sorry!'

Too late! She'd backed straight into someone with extremely long jean covered legs, strong tanned arms, and with enough presence of mind to hold on to her tightly from behind in order to prevent her ricocheting away and landing in an undignified heap on the floor.

''Orry — I 'ault,' said Bobbie through a mouthful of metal.

The arms gave a little, then gently turned her round. A pair of light denim, highly amused eyes looked into hers from what felt like a very great height. 'Well, I didn't quite catch that. But let me assure you no apologies are necessary. In fact any time you want to throw yourself around the place — well, I'm your man — for catching you, that is.'

Bobbie's keys dropped from her mouth and she felt a slow burning flush start at her feet and slowly make its way up to the top of her head. 'I said — Sorry, my fault,' she explained.

The arms did not relax their grip. Bobbie, together with the crushed watercolour paper and box of tubed paint, remained locked in place. The blue eyed giant showed no signs of wanting to move.

'Um, I'm all right now actually.'

'Right. OK. I'd better let go of you then.'

'Yes please.'

'OK. Yes, well I'll do that. Any second now.'

Bobbie felt his arms reluctantly loosen their grasp. 'I'm Roberta Armstrong,' she said breathlessly, because somehow she found she'd forgotten quite how to breathe. It was shock, that's what it was. It must be.

'Ah, then I'm one of your new students. My name's Charles, but I'm usually called Chas.'

Bobbie cleared her throat. 'Right,' she said struggling to be businesslike. 'Then I'll see you later, um, Chas. We all meet together at six-thirty for drinks and I give you a run down on the way we do things. You know, fire exits, the timetable and all that.'

'I'll look forward to it,' he said opening the barn door. 'Your colleague showed me my room. Now I'll just collect my baggage from my car.'

Charles seemed to expect her to say something — must be the way she was staring at him. She gave herself a shake. 'See you later then,' she managed.

With shaking hands she dumped the art materials in the studio then went straight to the office.

Mel looked up from entering details into the computer. 'What's up?' she asked, taking in Bobbie's flushed face and bright eyes.

'Well, nothing's up exactly. I just made a complete fool of myself by falling over a very early guest that's all.'

'Yes, what a piece of luck that was. He just called on the off chance. He's got a few days to kill, thought we were just B&B, but he's decided to attend the course as well.'

Bobbie turned away, because suddenly she felt a bit sick.

'Well, you might look a little more excited. We've filled the cancellation! Every room occupied. Lucky or what?'

'Yes, it's great,' agreed Bobbie mechanically, knowing that actually it wasn't great. That she didn't want this Chas person with his smiling blue eyes, his strong arms, and his way of looking at her as though he liked what he saw — she just didn't want him on her course at all.

The whole idea of it was, for some reason, very disturbing.

# 2

Chas had had no intention of joining the course. Just a couple of days B&B was all he'd been looking for.

He'd liked the look of the place all right. The large extended barn nestling in idyllic surroundings and the peacefulness that had washed over him as he stepped into the small but welcoming entrance lobby had immediately made him feel at home. The warmth with which Mel had greeted him, then her thinly-veiled disappointment when he'd explained that he was only after a couple of days respite, had made him change his mind about his initial *two days B&B then move on* plan, and sign up for the course.

After all, three days or so playing around with pens, pencils, paints and paper, might be very relaxing. Just the thing he needed. And goodness knows he had the right background. An architect by profession, he'd already done his share of building drawing, technical though it was. At least he would have no trouble with perspective.

Then, just as he'd finished signing; exactly on cue, as it were, an enchanting girl with pale brown hair and the bluest eyes he'd ever seen, had cannoned straight into him and the experience had been delightful. Furthermore, he'd discovered that she wasn't another student as he'd first thought, but was none other than Roberta herself — co-proprietor and the art tutor half of the establishment.

Chas lay full length on the bed of the room he'd been allocated and grinned at the memory of Bobbie's surprised expression. He supposed he wasn't the norm when it came to her usual students. He guessed they'd mainly be grey haired, female, and in their fifties. That must have been why her eyes nearly popped out of their sockets and he appeared to have difficulty in breathing.

The room he was in was quite plain. White walls, wooden floors with a blue and white kelim next to his bed, and blue checked curtains at the windows matching the duvet on which he was lying. There were three pictures on the walls. Two of them loose water colour washes over pen and ink drawings depicting boats in harbour, and one larger work of some rather exuberant nasturtiums. The scrawled signature — *R. Armstrong* in the corners, told him that, as he'd suspected, Roberta was the artist.

It all looked very promising. Yes, he could do with a few days break. This could be an ideal opportunity to unwind and recharge his batteries before moving on to the new job, a challenge, and who knew what else? The full line of his mouth took on a new firmness.

The last year had been hard. But he knew his decision, that it was time to stop being a prop for others to rely upon — to get away from his roots, was the right one. Now he was more than ready to start thinking about himself for a change and start planning his own future.

He glanced at this watch. Thanks to a good late breakfast, for once he wasn't hungry. The class were to meet at three for their first lecture — if lecture was what you could call it. That meant he had a couple of hours to get some shut eye in. Remembering Bobbie's bright eyes and flushed cheeks and delightful fluster, Chas grinned. Not quite what he'd expected of a genteel water colourist — not what he'd expected at all. The lecture might be fun.

It didn't take long to unpack his bag and hang up a couple of pairs of chinos and a few shirts. Contentedly, Chas spread his long body back out on the checked duvet, let out a long sigh and closed his eyes.

Roberta felt oddly nervous. Impatiently, she gave herself a mental shake.

Surely she'd been doing this job long enough to know that once she got started on her introduction to the course speech, she would be fine. If necessary, she was sure she could do it blindfolded now, should the unlikely need arise, but she admitted to herself that it wasn't the 'oh dear what if I forget what to say' type of nervousness she was suffering from.

It was more a tingling of anticipation, a sensation of excitement as to what the next moment would bring. And she had a sneaking suspicion that it could be the thought of her new pupil, the one with the clear blue eyes and the white teeth (it certainly wasn't the bald-headed vicar), that was the cause.

She giggled out loud then, glimpsing her reflection, the smile on her lips died. It was quite a while since she'd caught sight of her eyes sparkling with amusement and her mouth curving slowly upwards. For a long moment she stared into the mirror. Her eyes blue and once again serious, looked back.

This Chas character is a guest, she told herself. A PG — a student. He's probably married with six children. He'll be gone in four days, and anyway you, Roberta Armstrong, are not interested.

Glad to have nailed that thought very firmly on her head, Bobbie picked up a comb and smoothed her hair. Then with a hand that was not entirely steady, she applied some lip gloss. That was better. She was fine, absolutely fine.

When Roberta arrived in the big barn, Mel was putting out cups and saucers on a large wooden tray.

'Sorry, I'm a bit late,' Bobbie apologised. 'Here, I'll see to the chairs.'

'Can I give you a hand?'

Bobbie knew without looking exactly who it was lounging in the doorway offering his help.

'Thanks very much, but I can manage, thanks.'

Mel shot her a look of mild surprise. They'd often discussed how wonderful

27

it would be if occasionally the guests were to help with the arranging of the chairs. 'If each person were to carry their own chair, it would make life so much easier,' Bobbie had often grumbled. And now here she was refusing a perfectly genuine offer.

'Well,' went on the irritating voice in the doorway. 'It's none of my business of course, but I'd say you're a bit pushed for time, so how about I put out this back row. Is it four rows or five you're aiming for?' Chas looked pointedly at the somewhat ragged assembly of chairs.

'Oh all right then,' Bobbie snapped ungraciously.

For the second time Mel stopped in her task of arranging biscuits on a blue patterned plate and looked across at her friend. 'That's very good of you, Chas. Thanks very much,' she amended. 'Bobbie's always a bit nervous at this stage.'

'No I'm not,' said Bobbie indignantly. 'I'm not nervous in the slightest

. . . Thanks for your help,' she added belatedly, realising that in what seemed like no time at all, Chas had organised four neat rows of chairs.

Chas treated her to a wicked grin. 'No trouble at all ma'am.'

The other students were by now, slowly filtering into the barn. Mel greeted them all warmly and served them with tea or coffee. At this stage Bobbie flipped through her notes on the running and programme for the course.

She stood at the front of the rows of chairs and slowly looked round at the surrounding faces. All except Chas, she knew only too well what he looked like.

Bobbie took a deep breath. 'First of all,' she started. 'I'd like to welcome you all to your holiday home and your workplace for the next few days . . . I say workplace, but of course it's enjoyment and relaxation you've come here for. However, I do hope that by the end of our time together you will feel as though you've gained from the experience as well as having had some fun . . . '

At this juncture, although she didn't mean to do it, she found herself staring straight into the clear gaze of Chas. He gave her a long, slow, wink.

How dare he? Bobbie felt her cheeks flushing and looked away hurriedly. Luckily, the well-practised format of her introduction to the course took over, but she knew that she went through the rest of the résumé, explaining the whereabouts of the paints and other materials, the events she had organised, and contingency plans for bad weather, on auto pilot.

'OK,' she wound up about twenty minutes later. 'If there are no more questions. I suggest I'll start with my first demonstration, which is a fairly basic run through on materials, types of brushes — the results you can expect to get from them and how to achieve different brush strokes.

'Also a brief run through on colour and the way that with water colour we usually work from light to dark, using the white of our paper as white. I know most of you will already be aware of these things, but there's no harm in back tracking a little . . . '

The demo went well. Bobbie was pleased to find that all her students were enthusiastic, ready to listen but never the less eager to get started. Some of them, in particular Marjory, the vicar's wife, were already quite experienced and had come away in order to devote themselves to their hobby without interruption and to spend time with like-minded people.

Chas was the only fly in the ointment.

'Have you had much experience?' she asked him during her rounds of proper introduction.

Chas smiled a lazy smile, which told her three different things. One, that he liked her, two, that he was laughing at her, and three, that his experience was many and varied. She wasn't sure which of the three angered her the most.

'I'm an architect,' he said, 'by trade.'

'Ah.' He would be, she thought; knowing full well that the weakest part of her talent was perspective. 'That's very interesting. Not much I can teach you about perspective then is there?' She'd just have to change the venue with the challenging church roof to something she was more confident about. The boatyard perhaps?

'Oh, I don't know,' said Chas. 'I think there's probably a lot you could teach me,' his eyes twinkled. 'My colour theory is none existent, and my drawing skills are limited to buildings, buildings, buildings. Can't do New Forest ponies and as for people — I don't have a clue.'

Bobbie smiled sweetly. 'Well, you know your strengths and weaknesses, that's a good start,' she said preparing to move on to the next pupil.

'No chance of any extra tuition, I suppose?'

The smile became slightly fixed. 'No time unfortunately, Chas. So I'm afraid that's impossible.'

The class broke up at five and dinner was served at six-thirty. Roberta made use of the time to write brief notes about each student, in so far as she could remember, so that the next day she would have a basis to start from. That done, she briefly tidied the studio, made sure she had the correct paints and brushes to hand for tomorrow's demo, then made her way to the kitchen where Mel was putting the finishing touches to a large open dish of salad.

Bobbie stood for a few moments fiddling with the cups and saucers which lay ready for after dinner coffee. Thoughtfully Mel glanced across at her friend.

'Nice bunch, I thought.'

'Huh,' said Bobbie reaching across for a tea towel and polishing a spoon that really didn't need it.

'Well, that didn't sound very enthusiastic.'

'No, I suppose not, sorry. Oh, I'm

sure they're fine. It's just . . . '

'Just what?'

'Oh, nothing.'

Mel smiled the sort of knowing smile that drove Bobbie mad.

'What are you looking so smug about?'

'Your reservations wouldn't have anything to do with Chas would they?'

Bobbie polished the spoon with more force than was necessary. 'Chas? Chas who? Oh, him.'

'Yes, him,' Mel said in a voice which was beginning to sound exasperated. 'Him with the attractive eyes and the nice smile. That Chas.'

Bobbie had the grace to grin. 'Well yes, I suppose he does get up my nose a bit.'

By now Mel was openly laughing.

'What's so funny?'

'You . . . Honestly, the first time a dishy-looking man turns up and you scuttle away like a frightened rabbit. Come on, admit it. He is pretty dishy?'

'You know, for an old married

34

woman you're terrible! You've no business noticing dishy men.'

'So he is dishy then. You've just admitted it.'

'Not that dishy,' Bobbie stopped, a wicked smile curving her lips. 'Unless you compare him to the bald vicar, of course. And further more I've no intention of scuttling anywhere like a rabbit, frightened or otherwise. Now, is my dinner ready so I can take it to my warren and eat it in peace?'

Mel opened the oven door. 'What d'you fancy quiche or salmon? Or maybe I can tempt you to a bit of both?'

An appetising smell wafted up from the oven. Bobbie groaned. 'You make it so hard to say no. It looks delicious. A little bit of the salmon please and a tiny, tiny piece of quiche, oh and a few new potatoes and I'll take a bit of salad, shall I?'

Mel smiled. 'Well at least this guy hasn't affected your appetite. No, don't take that salad — I've just spent ages making it pretty — ours is in this left over bowl here.'

'I don't know,' grumbled Bobbie taking the laden tray from Mel. 'Work my fingers to the bone I do, and all I get is leftovers.'

'You love it,' said Mel. 'Now I'll give you fifteen minutes to eat that, then I'll dish up for the PGs and once I've served the coffees, I'll be on my way.'

Bobbie nodded. This arrangement suited them both. It left Mel free to go home and spend the evening with Tom, and Bobbie liked to eat her lunch and evening meal away from the guests, but never minded stacking the dishwater when the meal finished.

Occasionally, if she felt there was some lonely soul loitering about in the main room, she'd spend some time with the PGs after dinner, but usually she was too tired to do more than read or watch the television for the rest of the evening.

She took her tray through to her small sitting-room and poured herself a small glass of wine. Just as she sat down and was about to start eating she heard a peal of laughter coming from the area where the PGs were gathering in anticipation of dinner. There was a pause. Bobbie picked up her knife and fork. Then there was another howl of combined laughter.

Staring hard at the blank television screen, Bobbie mechanically began to eat. I like eating alone, she told herself. Yes, after a hard day's work, relaxing was the order of the day. What bliss it was to just be alone, collect your thoughts, and unwind.

Another gale of laughter floated up. Resolutely, Bobbie picked up the remote control. Time to watch the news, catch up on the day's events.

She wasn't lonely. No. Not in the slightest.

# 3

The guests had usually finished eating by seven-thirty. Coffee and the remains of the bottles of wine were left on the sideboard on a help yourself basis, but by about eight, Bobbie judged it to be time she could go down and finish the clearing up.

She was right, the dining area was deserted. No Chas, winking or otherwise. Only the two teachers were left in the sitting area. One of them was busily engaged with a crossword, the other leafing through one of the many books on art which Bobbie left out for reference. She hoped that particular teacher wasn't planning any trick questions later.

'Enjoy your meal?' Bobbie directed the question in the general direction of the two of them.

'Delicious,' said one.

'Very tasty indeed,' said the other, hardly glancing up from her crossword.

'Good.'

It didn't take long to clear the table, and the kitchen had been left spotless. Bobbie checked the fridge to see if there was any of her favourite frangipan tart left, in which case she would treat herself because she felt somehow that she'd had a trying day and she deserved it. No, no tart. What was the betting that winking Chas had eaten the last slice? Feeling slightly miffed, Bobbie shut the fridge door.

How dare he wink at her when she was in the middle of a very serious introductory speech? He could have put her off totally, made her make a complete mess of it. She'd have to watch out for him.

That was probably what all the laughing was about. He'd probably been making a joke at her expense. Well, winking Chas had just better watch out; she was on his case now. If he thought he could come here and poke fun at her well, he could think again.

Mechanically Bobbie folded the last tea towel and went to lock the back door. It would be sunset soon, and then twilight and she'd lock the back door, the studio door and the door to her flat.

The PGs all had a master key to their wing and could lock their individual doors from the inside, so those who'd ventured down the three hundred yard lane to the nearest pub, could just come back when they were ready. She could have an early night with the television as she had planned.

Force of habit made her open the back door and glance round the garden. Her eye fell on the green bucket where the vegetable peelings were kept for recycling on the compost heap way down at the bottom of the garden. It was so full the lid wouldn't close properly.

Knowing from experience that if she didn't empty it, the foxes would distribute its contents all over the garden, Bobbie stepped out of the back door and picked the bucket up.

It was a beautiful evening. The buds on some of the fruit trees looked ready to burst and the air was filled with the scent of daffodils. Bobbie took her time wandering down the curling path noticing as though for the first time, the freshness of the spring grass and the sound of the blackbird that was perched on the weather vein giving voice to his feelings.

She smiled to herself. 'OK, Mr Blackbird, I take your point.'

She was alive and should be grateful. Well, she was grateful. She was happy too. Well, content, anyway. Why then this feeling of restlessness, of something being missing?

She pulled the old sheet of floor covering off the compost heap and emptied the vegetable peelings and old bits of salad on to the top, before covering it again. Then she stood and looked back at the barn bathed as it was in the evening light. It looked warm and inviting.

She wandered back up the garden path and replaced the bucket outside the kitchen door.

On impulse, instead of going back inside, she carried on round the side of the barn and suddenly all the air was knocked out of her and for the second time that day she found herself imprisoned in a vice like grip by a pair of strong arms.

For a moment she was powerless to move. She could feel a thudding sensation and it took a moment for her to realise it wasn't her heart that was banging against her ribs — it was his and in that crazy instant she wanted to stay like that locked in this warm, and somehow comfortable, embrace for ever.

It was only an instant though, and definitely crazy. As soon as she was able to think straight, Bobbie pushed at the chest she was being held against and managed to free herself. A pair of light blue eyes twinkled down at her.

'Whoops, we'll have to stop meeting like this.'

Bobbie took some deep breaths. They were still standing very close and it was — well, it was unsettling. 'That was a bit cheesy, even for you,' she managed eventually.

Chas's eyes crinkled with amusement. 'Yes, I apologise. Lost my cool for a moment there. But then it's not every day that a beautiful woman throws herself at me, not once, but twice.

'Per-lease. I'm not beautiful and I certainly didn't throw myself at you. I just wasn't looking where I was going.'

'And where were you going?'

'Nowhere much.'

'Ah. Well, me? I was very definitely going somewhere.'

'What? To find the compost heap? That's where I've just been.'

'No, to find you and to ask you to show me where the nearest pub is.'

'I already gave all of you directions.'

'I know, but I'm not good at finding my way.'

Bobbie's eyes narrowed. 'Now, why don't I believe you?'

'I can't think.'

There was a long silence during which Bobbie noticed the directness of his gaze, the kindness of the curve of his mouth, and the very strength of his presence.

His expression became more serious. 'Please, Bobbie,' he said. 'I don't like drinking on my own. Not that I intend to get plastered,' he added hurriedly. 'But it would be really nice if you'd let me buy you a beer. Or an orange juice, or water if you prefer.'

Bobbie looked at him for another long moment. He's only here for three days, she thought. Where can the harm be?

'OK,' she said suddenly. 'But I'm a dry white wine girl.'

Chas had enjoyed his dinner, but he'd been disappointed that the guests had eaten separately from Bobbie, with Mel serving. He guessed Roberta preferred to eat alone, because he'd seen her sneaking off through a door marked *Private*, with a loaded tray.

He wondered if this was to be the same routine every evening. He thought it might be, and if he were to get to know her better, find out more about her and how her life worked — then he'd have to find some other way.

It was luck then, that as he took an after-dinner stroll around the barn looking at the structure from an architect's point of view more than anything, he just caught sight of her disappearing down the path with the vegetable peelings. He ducked round the edge of the building counted to ten and walked again towards the corner.

In three seconds flat she was in his arms again. And boy did she feel good? Steady Chas, don't get too carried away. You've only just met the girl, and OK so she's attractive and yes, there is definitely a spark between you, but her eyes are sad and right now involvement is not the plan.

But a drink, one little drink at the pub down the road. Now that could hardly be classed as a date. Chas watched as Bobbie's thought process obviously followed the same pattern.

Ten minutes later they were sitting facing one another at a corner table in the pub at the end of the winding lane. The atmosphere was noisy and friendly. Chas had had to fight to the bar and fight back again, avoiding an old lady with her shopping trolley and a sleeping dog, as he did so.

'Yep, it's pretty much always like this,' said Bobbie in answer to his question. 'More so, once the season really gets under way.'

'Well I like a crowded pub. Feels like home.'

Bobbie took a sip of her wine. 'And where's that?'

Chas hadn't meant to talk about himself, the idea, was to find out more about her. 'Oh, nowhere very interesting.'

'It can't be that bad. I think I can

detect a little bit of a northern accent.'

Chas grinned. 'No, Sheffield way, actually.' Chas took a sip of his beer. It was local and it tasted good. Bobbie seemed a little distracted. He thought, maybe he'd best change the subject.

'Well, how about you? Have you always lived in these parts?'

Bobbie gave herself a little shake and smiled. The radiance of the smile took him off guard, made him realise that she was more than attractive, where he was concerned anyway. 'Yes, I've lived here most of my life. My family have lived in Hampshire for generations. My mum and brother still do.'

'And the art thing? Has that been in the family too? Is it an inherited talent?'

Smiling again, Bobbie shook her head. 'No. I'm a one off. The rest of them are horsey people, but I always loved painting, ever since I can remember and I was one of the lucky ones in that I was encouraged from an early age. I went to teacher training college though, after my degree. Art alone is an overcrowded, not to mention difficult, profession.'

'I suppose it's like any of the arts; theatre, music, writing — you have to compromise in order to survive.'

Bobbie swirled her drink around in her glass. 'Well, I reckon I've found a pretty good compromise. I enjoy my job. I'm in surroundings I'm used to and that I love. I wouldn't want to live in the middle of London or any big city or town, come to that. I have to feel I'm within reach of the country. I'm very happy with my life.'

Chas watched her adamant face carefully. It was almost as though she was trying to convince herself not him. 'And what do you do besides?' he asked. Then as Bobbie continued to stare at him blankly. 'You know — in your spare time? For fun.'

'For fun?' she repeated after him as though trying to decide what fun was. Then her face brightened. 'Well, I have lots of friends. We go out together. I visit galleries. Visit family. You know, stuff like that. But I don't have an awful lot of time, because in the winter, although we don't do holidays, I still take classes — it's older people mainly but there was some talk of starting a Saturday club for kids. I'd like that.'

'Sounds great,' agreed Chas thinking all the same, that if it was so great, why did she have such an air of detachment and sadness about her?

'And of course, I paint for myself as well and sometimes manage to sell some.'

'The ones you have up in the barn? Yes, I noticed them, they're very good. There's one in my room I like particularly. It's of nasturtiums on a windowsill.'

'Ah, yes.'

'Are they all for sale?'

She gave him a mischievous glance from under her lashes. 'It's OK you don't have to buy anything. I just have them up in the hope that perhaps someone will like something enough to buy, but I never give it the hard sell.'

She shuddered. 'Not my style — not my style at all.'

Chas finished his drink. 'Ready for a refill?' he asked getting to his feet.

A shadow fell across the table. 'Hi, Bobbie. Thought you said you were too busy to come out tonight?'

Bobbie looked up at the large, fair pleasant-looking guy who'd appeared beside her. She looked as though she'd just had a nasty surprise. 'Oh Lee, hello,' she turned towards Chas. 'This is Chas, he's on the course.'

Chas found himself being examined by a pair of rather suspicious grey eyes. It gave him the feeling it wouldn't be a good idea to tread on this Lee character's toes.

'Hi Chas,' Lee said. 'Getting to know the area are you?'

'Yes, Bobbie was kind enough to show me the way to the nearest pub. I'm just about to get more drinks, can I get you anything?'

Lee hesitated for a moment, then shrugged. 'No, I'm here for the snooker. I'm on in a moment. Caught sight of you,' he said to Bobbie, 'thought I'd just check.'

Bobbie smiled the sort of patient smile mothers often bestow on their children. 'I'm fine thanks, Lee.'

'OK, I'll catch you later,' said Lee after a long moment of looking unconvinced.

Bobbie's faint sigh of relief reached Chas as he moved off towards the bar.

Two minutes later, Chas put two more drinks on the table. 'So, who's Lee?' he asked, although he'd spent his time waiting to be served telling himself he would, under no circumstances, ask that very question.

Bobbie sipped at her wine glass. 'Just a friend.'

Just a friend. The just was music to his ears.

'Actually,' went on Bobbie with a sigh. 'He's not just a friend. He's a very dear friend.'

Oh dear, well he should have guessed as much. No girl looking like Roberta looked, would stay alone for long.

'Why the sigh then?' he asked clutching at straws.

Bobbie flushed and glanced away. 'It'll sound big headed if I tell you.'

'Try me.'

'He's a good friend but, well, he wants me to go out with him and — you know . . . '

'No I don't. Why don't you go, if he's such a dear friend?'

The pub was really full now. There was the steady background murmur of conversation and then a sudden loud laugh. Chas had to bend closer to her to hear what she said.

'It's not as easy as that. I don't want to give him the wrong idea . . . I'm not in the market for a relationship.'

They looked at one another for what seemed a long time before Chas said, 'That's sad.'

An unpredictable fire started up in Bobbie's eyes. 'What d'you mean — that's sad — as though I'm some charity case or something? Why does everyone seem to think I can't be happy on my own?'

'Hold on,' answered Chas, a little thrown by this sudden attack. 'I meant it was sad for me not for you . . .'

'Oh.'

'Although on reflection, it's sad for you too. All work and no play . . . Seems such a shame. What brought it all on I wonder?'

'It's really none of your business.'

Chas laughed. 'Not very polite to your students, are you?'

'Sorry. I'm sorry. Look this probably wasn't a good idea. Business and pleasure never do mix.'

Blinking hard Bobbie picked up her glass and took a couple of sips. Chas stared at her downcast eyelids, at the way her hair fell across her cheek brushing her jaw bone. He noticed how tightly she was holding the glass and how tense was the line of her shoulders. He wanted to put an arm round her. Tell her everything was alright and she had no need to be sad.

Giving himself a mental shake, he cleared his throat. 'No, it's my fault. My trouble is, I find relationships fascinating. I think really I missed my true vocation — I should have been an agony aunt.'

Bobbie raised her eyes to his. 'I am relaxed now and I do thank you,' she said.

They talked about other things after that. Chas explained that he'd come down to start a new job in Bournemouth. That he was joining a team of architects and builders who worked for the local authority as well as themselves, on converting old buildings into senior citizen flats or luxury apartments. He wasn't due to start until the first of the month, but had already sold his flat in Sheffield. His new flat wouldn't become vacant for another week or so.

'Which gives me time to kill,' he finished. 'Which explains why I'm exploring the area.'

'What made you decide to take up

painting all of a sudden?' asked Bobbie curiously.

'Ah well,' said Chas. 'I've a feeling that if I told you that, you'd throw me off the course.'

'Well, Mel did say you'd only come in on the off chance of B&B for a couple of nights.'

Chas nodded. 'But of course, once I'd seen the set up, I was so impressed I just had to sign up.'

Bobbie looked at him suspiciously.

'And if you say you don't believe me again, I shall just have to tell you to mind your own business.'

The time had slipped by very quickly. Catching sight of her watch, Bobbie gulped down the remains of her drink. 'Well, thank you very much,' she said. 'I feel I really should be getting back now.'

'Wouldn't you like another?' asked Chas.

'Not if I want to get up in the morning. No, thank you very much. No, really I've had enough, but if you want to stay — that's fine. It's quite safe round here. I can walk back up the lane by myself.'

Chas glanced over towards the snooker area, where he'd noticed Lee was not really concentrating on the game, but was watching the progress of Bobbie's evening from under brooding eyebrows. 'No, I don't think so,' he said. 'I need to be on my metal tomorrow. I haven't put a brush to paper with any serious intent, for years.'

'Now who's taking life too seriously?' asked Bobbie.

# 4

It took Bobbie a long time to get to sleep that night, but she was no stranger to sleepless nights. For about six months after the climbing accident she'd thought she would never sleep a whole night through again. But eventually the wound to her heart, although not entirely healed, had begun to hurt less. The trick was, Bobbie discovered, to fill your day so full; you had no time to think.

The demanding work of restoring the barn and starting up the business had tired her mentally and physically, so that insomnia gradually became a thing of the past.

Till now. Willing herself to relax, Bobbie stared at the ceiling. It was no good, instead of the thick black velvet curtain she was meant to be visualising, a replay of the evening started in her brain.

Belatedly she told herself she should never have gone to the pub with him. Not that there was any hard and fast rule about not fraternising with the PGs. Many times last summer, a whole crowd of them had ended up at the same pub and spent a thoroughly enjoyable evening.

Restlessly, Bobbie turned over, trying to find a comfortable position for sleep. That was a crowd though. This evening was a twosome. Just Chas and herself facing one another across the rickety oak table — talking and laughing, enjoying each other's company.

Suddenly, Bobbie felt she'd burst if she didn't move. She pushed her cover back, swung her legs to the floor and went to fetch a glass of water.

She paused by a small pencil sketch she'd framed and hung on the wall in the corner of her sitting-room. It had been torn from one of her sketch pads and showed the back view of a man who could have been anyone, but Bobbie knew it was John. For some moments she stood contemplating the back of John's head, the jut of his cheekbone, the angle of the back of his ear, and the line of his shoulder under the ribbed sweater he was wearing. It was the only drawing she'd done of him that she felt captured his very essence.

From the angle of his head it was easy to imagine that his eyes were fixed on some distant horizon that beckoned beguilingly. At the time she'd resisted the urge to sketch the mountains in the background, but she might as well have done because she never looked at the picture without seeing them there — cruel, dark and menacing.

With a sudden movement she took the picture from the wall and placed it face down on the sideboard, and after another five minutes pacing round her small flat she put a fresh glass of water on her bedside table, punched her pillow and climbed back into bed.

Now where was she? Yes, there was no reason for her to worry. OK so Chas was nice, she'd admit that. Well yes, all right — Chas was more than nice, he was very nice. Not as good looking as Lee, when she came to think of it. His nose was a bit on the big side and his mouth when he smiled was lopsided — but on the other hand the smile itself was a most attractive smile.

Don't think about his mouth, she told herself sternly. Don't think about the way his eyes twinkled down at her or the feel of his hand on her back as he guided her back up the lane. She had to ignore the way her heart went pitter patter, when the barn was finally reached and she thought, for a terrible moment, that as he leaned towards her, he was going to kiss her.

What a relief to realise he was only reaching past her to unlock the door. It would have been awful if he had made a pass — just awful.

After another thirty minutes of assuring herself just how embarrassingly awful it would have been, at the same time wondering what exactly it would have felt like, Bobbie drifted into an uneasy sleep.

When the alarm clock went off the next morning Bobbie groaned and put her head under the pillow. It couldn't possibly be morning already; the last thing she remembered, and surely that could only have been five minutes ago, was the sound of the birds beginning to sing.

Twenty minutes later, after a hurried shower and an even more hurried selection of clothes, and faster than light make-up application, Bobbie was in the kitchen listening to a white faced Mel.

'The thing is, Bobbie, I know Danielle's baby isn't due for another two weeks, and Pete will be home by then, but I can't help worrying about her. She's been having twinges all night.'

'Has she called her midwife?' asked Bobbie setting a tray with jams, marmalades and the local honey.

Mel nodded. 'She said not to worry, first babies always take their time.'

'Well, I expect she knows best. Anyway,' she continued giving her friend's shoulders a squeeze. 'Loads of babies are born every day. I'm sure she'll be fine.'

'I know. I keep telling myself that. But somehow, now it's my sister giving birth it all seems a lot more worrying.'

Mel turned back to the cooker where she had neat lines of bacon lined up for grilling. She glanced at her watch. 'That can't be the time. They'll be down in a moment. Take that tray through to the sideboard quick!'

Bobbie did as she was told, and after making sure there was nothing else she could do to help, sat down at the kitchen table for her own breakfast of grapefruit, toast and tea. She preferred to eat alone when running the courses, in order to give herself time to think.

The morning had dawned fine and bright although the forecast threatened cloud and occasional rain later. The plan for the day was to visit Lymington with sketch books and cameras at the ready.

The mornings work of sketches and digital photos which, after lunch, could be loaded into the computer and printed out, were then to be used as reference later in the day when the students began work in the studio on their larger, watercolour composition.

Bobbie took four passengers in her car, and the vicar, Chas and the teachers volunteered to take the remainder in their cars. By the time they reached Lymington it was eleven o'clock so they had mid-morning coffee before walking down to the harbour. It was the beginning of the season and the harbour looked at its beautiful best, crammed to capacity with yachts of all shapes and sizes bobbing up and down on the sparkling water.

Once Bobbie had her students happily placed and settled, she drew their attention to the fact that the harbour was tidal so the yachts would twist and change direction together with the turning of the tide. It meant they would be advised to make several quick sketches, concentrate on shapes and horizontal lines rather than spend too much time on detail.

'Don't forget to note the direction the light is coming from, the wind direction, and write down the colours you want to use in your books too,' she finished.

The morning passed pleasantly enough. Bobbie moved between her students offering words of encouragement and advice where necessary. Chas was sitting near talkative Marjory, the vicar's wife who had got straight down to business and, by the time Bobbie reached her, had completed several small thumb nail sketches which Bobbie couldn't fault. Chas on the other hand, had completed one very draughtsman-like drawing of a yacht in cross section.

'Yes, very good,' said Bobbie.

'Go on, say what you really think,' encouraged Chas. 'Lacking imagination perhaps?'

Bobbie sneaked a look at him. He

was wearing a black sweater and jeans, and his dark hair was sticking up slightly at the back. She wondered whether maybe he'd had trouble sleeping too. 'I wouldn't say lacking imagination exactly. It's good. Extremely accurate, but it's almost a text book drawing. It doesn't have to be perfect. Try just going for an impression. Look at the varying tones, light against dark . . . The sails, when you look at them, are catching the wind, there's a whole lot of movement going on. Try to put that into your drawing.'

'Oh, I'm so discouraged,' said Chas in broken tones. 'Maybe I'll never paint again.'

Marjory looked up sharply.

'It's all right,' explained Bobbie hastily. 'That's Chas trying to be funny. I don't know why you came on this course if you're not going to take it seriously,' she said severely.

'Sorry, Teacher,' said Chas with a crestfallen expression, which was spoiled when he gave her a broad wink.

The weathermen were right, by one-thirty, just as they were packing up, the clouds rolled over and it was obvious they'd had the best of the day. The group had gelled nicely by now so on the car journey back to the barn the conversation flowed freely, and all Bobbie had to do was concentrate on her driving and how much she really didn't like Chas, although not necessarily in that order.

'OK. Lunch is at two-fifteen and I'll see you any time after three in the studio and we'll get stuck into some painting.' Bobbie went through to her flat to tidy up and then to the kitchen to find a grim-faced Mel staring into the open freezer.

'What's up?'

'Oh, thank goodness you're back. I don't know what to do. Danielle's twinges are now full blown labour pains. I've rung Pete and he's on his way — should get back by about seven, but they've taken Danielle into hospital.'

'Well, why are you still here? Go on. You have to be with her.'

Mel pulled out a pack of bolognese sauce. 'I know, I know. But I can't leave you in the lurch.'

'I'll manage.'

'Bobbie, that's sweet and I know you mean well but — you can't cook.'

Bobbie tried to look confident. 'I'm sure I can manage lunch.'

'Oh, I've done lunch, I'm not bothered about lunch. There's ham and chicken salad, and hot new potatoes and apple pie. They can help themselves off the sideboard as usual. It's dinner that's the problem, I can't promise I'll be back in time.' Mel ran her hands through her dark curls in despair.

'I can order in pizzas.'

'Brilliant!' Mel danced a jig round the table. 'Here,' she thrust the frozen bolognese sauce at Bobbie. 'You can heat this and the carbonara sauce on the side there, and boil tagliatelle as an alternative. There's more bags of salad in the fridge and tomatoes and peppers and stuff. Heat up some garlic bread as well. Pizzas were a brainwave — they'll have a choice. Wonderful! Thanks, Bobbie. I knew you wouldn't let me down. I was thinking of letting you defrost the fish pie, but I don't really trust you with that.'

'What d'you mean, you don't trust me?' said Bobbie indignantly.

'You'd serve it to them half frozen or dried out or something. No, you'll manage the sauce — much easier! You'll be fine. Got to dash. Tell the PGs they'll have an extra special breakfast and lunch tomorrow!'

Helplessly, Bobbie watched as Mel snatched up her bag and car keys and, with a last few hurried instructions regarding putting butter on the pot of new potatoes in the oven, and taking the meats and salad through to the dining-room; she disappeared out of the kitchen door.

'Give my love to Danielle,' Bobbie shouted after her. 'And let me know when she has it. Her, him, what-ever . . . '

Then she looked round the kitchen and wondered whether to have the nervous breakdown now or save it for when she had to single handedly provide dinner for seventeen people.

★   ★   ★

Chas had enjoyed the morning's lesson. He was quite pleased with his drawing of the yacht, and even more pleased that in the cold light of day his previous night's fears that he was getting in too deep, had dissolved.

Bobbie was a great girl. Good looking, pleasant company. The sort of girl you might like to settle down with some day. But not now, not today, now that last night's temporary loss of sanity had been well and truly overcome, he could breath easily again, watch her dispassionately, relax and enjoy himself.

Yes, he'd nearly blown it last night. Chas felt hot at the memory. It had seemed so natural as they walked back up the shadowy lane to take her arm, guide her over the rough ground, even though she probably knew every rut and puddle like the back of her hand. They had walked for a while in companionable silence. Then he'd pointed out the shape of the Plough in the sky and she in her turn had spotted the North Star.

They'd stood with their heads together in a curious sort of peace, contemplating the great navy sky. No doubt about it, it had been a good moment.

He supposed it must have been that feeling that triggered the later, ridiculous desire, when he'd bent towards her in order to open the heavy oak door to the PG's wing, to lean forward that little bit more and kiss her.

Madness, complete madness. Of course her proximity played a part. That, and the moonlight; because the urge was totally unpremeditated. One moment he was laughing softly at something she'd said and the next he was having to fight his every instinct not to take her gently by the shoulders, turn her towards him and kiss her very soundly on that sad, sweet mouth of hers.

He shook his head. That was a close call. It would have ruined everything. He congratulated himself on being sensible and resisting the urge. But never the less he had lain awake until the early hours just thinking about Bobbie.

The way her hair fell forward to brush her cheek, the straight set of her shoulders; the way, when she smiled her whole face lit up, and the sad expression in her eyes when her face was in repose and she thought no-one was watching.

What a relief then to find in the morning, that Bobbie had returned once again, to being that efficient, attractive girl, the art teacher. Chas could cope with that.

The format for lunch was a *help*

*yourself* buffet which he was surprised to note Bobbie seemed to be in charge of. Aware that he was a little late, he took the last seat at the table with a murmured apology.

'No Mel?' he asked with raised brows.

'No. There's been a bit of a family emergency,' explained Bobbie. 'Luckily, she'd finished preparing the lunch though and she might be back before dinner.'

Everyone appeared to be very hungry after their morning's activities and the food disappeared fast. Even Marjory didn't have much to say, other than to praise the food in a voice most people would describe as a shout, but which Chas had come to realise that, for her, was normal.

Bobbie ate at the dining-table with them. Chas guessed she thought it would save time, as she surely had to rethink her schedule without Mel's backup. Chas was the last one to finish, he'd told the others not to wait and they'd gone through to the studio already.

'I'll be through in about five minutes,' called Bobbie after them.

Chas stood up. 'You go on through now — get them started,' he said. 'I can clear this lot and get them in the dish washer.'

Bobbie hesitated. 'That's really kind of you Chas, but . . . '

'But what? You're scared I'll break the plates. I won't I promise. I used to be a plate spinner you know. That was before I was an architect or an agony aunt. I was very good . . . Never broke one. That's better,' he added, as a smile tugged at the corners of her mouth. 'Now go on, and stop looking so worried. You're doing a great job. I'll expect extra tuition when I catch you up mind.'

It didn't take long to clear the plates. Any left over food had already been stored away in the fridge by Bobbie. Chas looked round the spotless kitchen. There was no doubt about it, they had a well set up enterprise going here.

Chas stood in respectful silence as he imagined the work involved in keeping the place running as smoothly as it did. It would only take one of them to be ill at the wrong time or something unexpected to happen for the whole thing to grind to a halt. No wonder Bobbie looked anxious.

The afternoon's session in the studio was not what Chas would call successful. Not from a painting point of view anyway. He either seemed to use too much water or not enough.

His sky was OK he supposed, if rather too blue, but the water that started off not bad every time he worked on it, just got muddier.

'Less is more,' said Bobbie enigmatically when he asked for help. 'I suggest you flood it with water and blot it off. Leave it to dry, then try a few dry brush strokes in a brownish tone later. I'd suggest an ultramarine mixed with light red.'

'Red?' questioned Chas. 'Has some-one been murdered on board?'

'It won't look red. It'll just dull the blue a little. Just try it will you, and stop arguing.'

Hmm. So she was bossy too. Chas grinned and did as he was told.

At the end of the session, Bobbie left them to continue for as long as they liked while she went to make prepara-tions for dinner, which was to be at seven-thirty. Chas cleaned up straight away and went to find her in the kitchen.

He stuck his head round the door. 'How're you doing, Della?'

'Ha ha, very funny.' Bobbie was sitting at the table reading the instruc-tions on the pasta packet. 'How on earth does Mel do all this?' she asked in an agonised voice. 'Pasta for seventeen — I ask you. I'm going to need three of these great big pans for the pasta and we've only got two, then I need another two rings and smaller pans for the pasta and we've only got two, then I need another two rings and smaller pans for the sauces. How am I going to watch it all at once, and get the salad and garlic bread ready, and order the pizzas? The timings are never going to be right. I'm going to ruin everything.'

'No you won't. We'll manage.'

'It's all very well for you to say that. You've never tasted my raw toad in the hole, or my other speciality, burnt shepherds' pie . . . ' Her face brightened. 'I know — I could take them all down to the pub, the food there's good.'

Chas could see two lots of sauce out on the counter. He shook his head. 'It'll cost you a fortune. Anyway, you've got all the ingredients here. The pasta sauce is homemade isn't it? It looks great. What's this? Bolognese right? And this is carbonara? Terrific! There's only the salad to do — that's easy. Even you can do that. Now it's not unreasonable to ask everyone ahead, which they would prefer of whether they'd like pizza — just give them a choice of two pizzas.

We'll be fine I promise . . . Anyway, didn't I mention . . . '

Bobbie held up her hands. 'No don't tell me. Let me guess. You used to be a chef, right?'

# 5

Despite Bobbie's misgivings, the evening meal was a great success. By nine o'clock that evening she was quite ready to admit that this was more due to Chas than to herself. Somehow he'd managed to make the whole thing into fun. The other guests had joined in with the spirit of the thing and pretty soon with the help of two extra bottles of wine, which she felt Mel would allow under the circumstances, the atmosphere became almost party like.

True, there had been one moment of panic when they both realised that they'd been so busy thinking about the pasta, Parmesan and plonk, that they'd forgotten about pudding.

'Sorry, don't do puddings,' said Chas. 'Never have done. Cheese and biscuits or fresh fruit and ice-cream in our house.'

'That'll do. Excellent.'

Bobbie hastily arranged a selection of cheeses and crackers on a large wooden board which she thrust into Chas's hands. Then she retrieved some chocolate sauce and a large catering-sized jar of fruits of the forest and as an afterthought a hand of bananas. The tub of ice-cream with a selection of toppings went down very well. After that, not many of them had room for cheese and biscuits or coffee.

When the guests eventually managed to stagger away from the table, Chas and Bobbie were left with the debris of the meal, a half burnt candle and the tail end of a bottle of wine. Feeling suddenly at a loss for words, Bobbie sat down next to him at the table and topped up their glasses.

'Cheers,' she said, finally looking Chas in the eyes. 'Uh, well . . . Here's to you. Thanks for your help. I um, I couldn't have managed without you.'

His eyes smiled into hers. She noticed that although they were so light as to be icy blue, the outer rim of the iris was almost purple, it was so dark. The combination was arresting, to say the least.

'Here's to teamwork,' he said. 'Your second course was superb. I thought the vicar would die from excitement, that or a chocolate sauce overdose.'

'The ice-cream was homemade. By Mel, of course — I wouldn't know how to start. I hope it wasn't being saved for a special occasion.'

'Well, I'd call this special . . . You've just coped with feeding the five thousand.'

'Seventeen actually, but you're right. I can hardly believe it.' She lowered her eyes. 'Mainly down to you, though. You're a good cook. I mean the timing and all that. How come?'

Chas grinned. 'Had to in our family.'
'Why?'

'No women . . . Well, after I was twelve, anyway. Mum had arthritis — really bad. Couldn't do much really, for years.'

Bobbie bit her lip. 'I'm sorry. That's sad.'

Chas took another sip of wine. 'We weren't sad, not really. It wasn't good to see her in pain, but most of the time she kept cheerful and she liked us to be cheerful, too.'

'So was it just you and your dad then?'

'No, I've got two brothers. I'm the eldest.'

It couldn't have been an easy childhood. Bobbie swallowed. Imaginary pictures of Chas arriving back from school and starting to prepare dinner before his dad came home from work, came into her mind. But one look at his face told her sympathy was the last of his requirements.

She knew that feeling only too well. 'Oh, so that's what makes you bossy,' she said quickly.

Chas looked injured. 'Moi? Bossy? That's rich coming from you. Anyway, I'm not bossy ... Just get on with clearing this table — why don't you?'

In the middle of taking the last sip from her wine glass, Bobbie laughed — then the laugh turned into a splutter and the wine shot down her nose in a very unladylike fashion.

Amidst all the coughing and spluttering, she thrust her drink on to the table, knocking Chas's glass over with a clatter. The next thing she knew, Chas was patting her on the back none too gently and mopping up the wine from her front with far more attention than was necessary.

'I'm all right, thanks,' she gasped. 'No, really, I'm fine.'

'Well, your T-shirt's soaked.'

Bobbie's face flushed. 'What is it with you?' she asked. 'I seem to turn into a walking accident every time you're around.'

Chas looked crestfallen. 'Sorry,' he said. 'But at least I made you laugh. That's probably it. You haven't laughed for such a long time, your throat's just not used to it.'

He mopped up the spilt wine and set

his glass to rights. 'Oh, dear, all gone. I was looking forward to that. Didn't have time at the meal what with one thing and another.'

Bobbie immediately felt guilty. 'I'm so sorry,' she said apologetically. 'You're a PG and I'm treating you like the hired help. I'll get you another bottle — it's the least I can do.'

'Don't be daft,' said Chas. 'I'm not a raving alcoholic. I can survive for one night without a drink . . . Now come on, let's clear up.'

In the event, it was Chas who did most of the clearing up because just then the phone rang, and on the end was a wildly relieved Mel telling Bobbie that she now had a niece called Amelia, who was the sweetest, most wonderful little miracle that had ever happened.

Bobbie was delighted and as enthusiastic about hearing all the details as it was possible to be, whilst being aware that Chas, once more, was doing all the work — which meant she would be even more in his debt and Bobbie knew if there was anyone whose debt she didn't want to be in, it was his.

When eventually Mel had run out of baby news, she asked how the evening meal had gone and for no good reason, Bobbie found herself reluctant to explain that something she'd been dreading all afternoon had turned into a weird kind of special occasion. 'I managed,' she said, 'but I did have a lot of help . . . the PGs were great. We had your special ice-cream for pudding. I hope that was OK? And I think we used more wine than usual. I'm not so good at keeping the brake on that kind of thing as you are.'

'You're a star. I told you, you could do it. I'll see you for breakfast.'

Still clutching her mobile phone, she was just about to go through the door marked Private, which was the door to her flat, when Chas came towards her from the direction of the kitchen.

'All done,' he said.

Awkwardly, they stood facing one another. 'That was Mel.'

'I gathered.'

'Yes, her sister's had her baby. It's a little girl. She sounded — thrilled.'

'That's good.'

'Yes, isn't it?'

'Well, what are you going to do now?'

'Um, look. I've got a bottle of champagne in the fridge. It's been there since my birthday. Perhaps you'd like that — as a thank you,' she added in case he thought — well, what did she care what he thought?

'Sounds good,' Chas said again. 'Specially if you share it with me.'

With her hand on the doorknob, Bobbie contemplated for a moment. She was a big girl. Surely she could share a friendly glass of champagne with someone who had saved the reputation of Painter's Barn?

'OK,' she said, opening her door. 'Come in.'

Thank goodness the flat was tidy. Not that she cared what he thought, of course. She went through to the tiny cupboard she called a kitchen, and opened a small fridge where the champagne had sat for too long, probably. She brought it back into the sitting-room together with two glasses.

'Now, you can figure out how to open it while I just change my T-shirt.'

Back in her bedroom, Bobbie peeled off her T-shirt and looked for something suitable to put on. Another T-shirt was the obvious choice, but having dismissed anything with a neckline that could be considered remotely low, the remainder all appeared a bit on the boring side. Not that she was trying to impress him. Goodness no. Why would she want to do to that?

Eventually she settled on a pink, roll necked, ribbed cotton sweater she knew suited her, but could never be described as femme fatal looking. It wouldn't do to make him think she was interested in him, because she wasn't. Sharing a bottle of champagne meant nothing, absolutely nothing.

Taking a deep breath and squaring her shoulders, Bobbie stepped into the sitting-room. Chas was standing examining the small pencil sketch of John that she had left face down on her sideboard.

Bobbie stood as though frozen to the spot. What did he think he was doing? How dare he?

He must have heard her sudden intake of breath because he swung round to face her. His expression was unfathomable.

'Sorry,' he said. 'Have I touched a nerve or something? You look as though you've seen a ghost.'

Quickly, Bobbie pulled herself together and flashed him a smile. 'Haven't you opened the champagne yet? I thought you were a whiz at all things culinary?'

Chas didn't put the picture down. 'No, I got sidetracked. Who's this?' He indicated the picture.

Bobbie picked up the corkscrew, then put it down again. 'No-one much,' she said with a shrug. 'Now, what d'you have to do with this? Twist the wire off somehow, don't you?'

Chas was still studying the drawing. 'No-one much,' he repeated. 'Now, you surprise me. I would have said this drawing has been executed with such sensitivity that you'd have to know the subject very well . . . '

'Not necessarily,' Bobbie replied in an icy voice.

She turned back to him and concentrated very hard on the champagne bottle. 'You'd think they'd put instructions on how to open this, wouldn't you?' she continued in a bright tone. 'I mean, it's not every day you open a champagne bottle, at least not in my lifetime it isn't . . . '

Her voice petered out, and there was a long silence.

'It's not a crime to care for someone, you know.'

'Pardon?'

'You heard what I said . . . '

Bobbie was tight-lipped. 'Yes, I heard. I couldn't quite believe it, that's all. What right have you got to start telling me what I should think or how I should behave? I know you helped out tonight and I'm grateful, but that doesn't give you the right to stick your nose into my private affairs or criticise my work or my life and the way I choose to live it.'

After carefully replacing the picture face down on the sideboard, Chas lifted his hands in the air and smiled his familiar white-toothed smile. 'OK. I'm sorry. I was out of line.'

Bobbie was still shaking. 'Yes, you were,' she said. 'And now I think it's best if you go. I've got a long day tomorrow and to tell you the truth, I'm too tired to even think about drinking champagne.'

Chas took a step towards her. 'Sometimes it helps to talk to a stranger.'

'What? What on earth are you on about now? I don't need to speak about anything to anyone. And even if I did — it certainly wouldn't be to you. Although you're certainly strange — I'll give you that . . . You — ' Bobbie lost track of what she was going to say next because there was the sudden strident sound of the back door bell followed by a voice calling from the kitchen area.

'Who on earth is that?' asked Bobbie of no one in particular. 'I must have forgotten to lock the back door.'

What was the matter with me? Bobbie thought to herself in fury. Inviting men into her own private area to drink champagne; forgetting to lock the back door? She'd better get a grip before she messed up the quiet, orderly life she'd grown so used to.

'Hi, Bobbie.' Lee was just inside the kitchen door.

Bobbie heaved a sigh of relief. 'Hello, Lee. Sorry. I was in my flat, didn't hear you call.'

Lee was looking at her strangely. She realised she was breathing fast and that her colour was probably heightened. Usually she would strive to appear pretty cool around Lee, that way she could stay in control.

'You look a bit frazzled. I met Tom in

the pub. He told me you were coping here on your own because Mel's sister has just had a baby. I came to see if you needed a hand.'

Unaccountably, Bobbie felt tears at the back of her eyelids. 'That's really sweet of you, Lee. But as you see, I seem to have managed . . . '

'Well, you look exhausted.' Lee carried on staring at her as though there was something he couldn't quite understand.

It was better to go along with him than argue. 'Well, yes, I suppose I am a bit tired.'

A small cough sounded behind her and Chas sauntered into the kitchen. Trust him, thought Bobbie, always poking his nose in. Now this was going to get even more complicated than it was already.

'I was just about to make some coffee for a guest who helped out. Oh, you've met Chas already, haven't you? Come on in and join us.'

Lee pulled out a chair. 'Right.'

The two men stared at each other for a long moment then Chas sat down on the edge of the table and swung his legs. 'How did the snooker go?'

Only half listening to the ensuing conversation about breaks and pockets and all things snookerish, Bobbie busied herself with making the coffee. Why did she feel so guilty? She had nothing to feel guilty about. It wasn't as if she and Chas were doing anything wrong, it wasn't as if she'd planned to entertain him with an evening of champagne and seduction. It wasn't as if she even liked him.

Huffily, she stood with her back to them, wiping a sink that was already sparkling, and waiting for the coffee to brew. Her euphoric mood of earlier had changed to one of weary depression. She couldn't wait for both men to drink their coffee and leave her in peace.

However, it was a good half hour later that Chas stood up, said he should be getting his beauty sleep and left Bobbie and Lee in the kitchen.

'I should go too,' said Lee, his good-looking face breaking into a smile which was pleasant, but did not quite evoke the same response in her as Chas's white-toothed grin.

'Well, I am rather tired,' agreed Bobbie, yawning to prove it.

'Well, I'm glad you managed OK. Look, if ever something like this happens again, give me a call. I'll always help — you know that.'

'Thanks, Lee. I just didn't think of it. It was all such a rush. I took the class to Lymington this morning, then when I got back, I had to serve lunch. Then I had to supervise in the studio, do afternoon teas and coffees. Next thing I knew, dinner was upon us. I tell you, I didn't realise how much organisation was needed. Mel makes it look easy.'

'Yes, well,' Lee was looking at her searchingly. 'I gather this Chas character stepped into the breach.'

'Not exactly, but he helped out, yes.' It was strange how defensive she felt about Chas, considering she didn't know him too well. 'Not that I couldn't have managed without him, the timings would have been a bit off, that's all.' Suddenly she laughed and pushed her hair back behind her ears. 'Who am I trying to kid? It would have been a disaster. He was brilliant.'

Lee opened the back door. 'Brilliant, was he? That's good. OK, I'm off. Don't forget what I said. And bolt the door when I've gone.'

Bobbie allowed Lee to give her a brotherly hug which excited her not one iota, and when he'd gone, did as she was told and locked the door.

Yawning widely, she made her way back to her flat. Her earlier anger had evaporated. Chas had been great. They'd worked comfortably together. In spite of the hard work, the evening had been fun. Until he'd seen the drawing of John.

The picture. She picked it up from the sideboard and remembered for a painful moment what it had been like to run her finger down the side of his cheekbone. Remembered the roughness of that very sweater against her skin. Her eyes darkened with the pain of it. No, it hadn't gone away. She was a fool to think it ever would.

But before she went to sleep that night, she wondered what it would have felt like to confide in Chas. To tell him everything and let herself be comforted.

# 6

Chas woke up with a heavy head. The first thought that came into his mind was that somehow he had to talk to Bobbie. It was the last full day of the course and he knew for sure now that although he wasn't convinced he wanted to pursue watercolour painting as a hobby, he certainly didn't want to lose contact with Bobbie.

Just a friendship, he told himself. After all that was all she wanted, all she seemed ready for. Tomorrow he had to visit the launderette on his way to spend a further week with friends in Southampton, before picking up the keys to his new flat. Not good to turn up to stay, with a suitcase of dirty washing.

Yes, he had a busy time ahead. Very busy. No time to dally with romance, even if Bobbie was the dallying type, which she clearly was not. But staying in touch for friendship's sake — surely there'd be no objection to that?

He showered, sorted his washing out — putting it altogether in a plastic bag, tidied the rest of his belongings and was just tucking his shirt into his jeans when his mobile rang.

Flicking the phone open, he could see it was his middle brother ringing. Well, that figured. Frowningly, Chas looked at his watch. He should be having breakfast now. His brother would just have to wait; he'd call back later.

Sniffing with appreciation at the aroma of sizzling bacon in the air, Chas went to find his breakfast. He remembered that after they'd eaten they were to watch a demonstration on working from a photograph and changing the time of day depicted in the photograph. Although; why anyone should want to do that, Chas couldn't imagine.

As he passed the studio, he caught an unexpected glimpse of Bobbie who was busy sorting through materials and setting up her easel. At the sight of her slender frame, topped by her swinging hazelnut hair, a strange sensation made itself felt in the region of his chest. It was almost as though his heart had stopped beating for a few seconds, then started again at a much faster rate than normal.

What a ridiculous idea. That stuff was only for the heroines of romantic fiction. That kind of thing didn't happen to a twenty-nine-year-old architect on the verge of a new business venture.

With some difficulty, Chas tore his eyes away from Bobbie's struggle with her easel and resisted the impulse to burst through the studio door and come to her aid. Instead he dutifully followed his nose to the breakfast which, a moment earlier, had beckoned so tantalisingly.

He decided that perhaps he was a little feverish, because for once in his life he couldn't finish his bacon and eggs. In vain he tried to emulate interest in the conversation buzzing round him. Luckily, because it was dominated by the subjects of Mel's new baby niece, it was easy for him to play an audience only role.

'The time's gone so fast, hasn't it?' hooted Marjory in his left ear. 'I expect you'll be glad to get away from all us women tomorrow, I know Geoffrey will.'

Chas smiled uncertainly before remembering that Geoffrey was the vicar.

'Geoffrey was so pleased when he spotted you on the course. He was convinced he'd be the only man here and the time would drag, but now, well, in spite of being outnumbered, he's enjoyed himself so much — I don't think he wants the course to end really.'

Chas smiled again, aware that he echoed Geoffrey's sentiments, but probably for very different reasons.

'The rooms are lovely and clean, the food's delicious. And she's so sweet

— Roberta, Bobbie, I mean,' went on Marjory. 'And so very talented too, but she never makes you feel stupid, does she? It's been such an excellent course, I said to Geoffrey, I wouldn't mind coming again — I really wouldn't.'

Nodding weakly, Chas wondered what on earth was wrong with him. He didn't seem to be able to think straight. He should be itching to get away, to get on with his life. Not mooning about putting off the moment of departure. Lovesick and teenager were the two words, which sprang to mind.

'Good morning everyone.' Bobbie had arrived without him hearing her and now stood at the end of the table smiling and pushing her hair back behind her ears in a gesture that had played behind his eyelids all night, come to think of it. 'Sorry the weather's not up to much.' For the first time that morning, Chas realised that outside there was a steady drizzle. 'I plan to get started in about five minutes,' carried on Bobbie.

'We'll work right through till lunch, then after lunch hopefully the sun is promised and I'll take you outside to sketch some of the trees round about, until fourish but naturally, you can come in at any time and use the studio for as long as you like.'

Her glance swept over the table's occupants, Chas wondered if her eyes locked on his just a fraction too long or whether he'd imagined it. With a final smile Bobbie headed for the studio closely followed by the other guests.

For this particular class, Chas sat near the back. He watched as Bobbie became more and more absorbed in her work, showing how the same picture could take on the mantle of a fresh frosty morning, the languid humidity of a summer afternoon, or the rosy glow of sunset; all with a change of underlying washes and light direction.

Marjory was right, Bobbie was very talented and very sweet. Altogether the kind of girl you didn't come across every day.

The demo was coming to an end. It was time for the students to work from a photograph of their own or to choose, from one of the many Bobbie had provided in neatly labelled shoe boxes. Street Scenes, Trees and Woods, Buildings in Landscapes, Boats and Beaches.

No mountains then.

'You OK, Chas? You look as though you're in shock or something?'

It was one of the teachers. Aware that he was in danger of turning into a smiling moron, Chas smiled vaguely yet again and tried to concentrate.

Eventually he chose a photo from the Buildings in Landscape box, set up his work station, then stared at his blank sheet of paper.

'You're a bit quiet, Chas.' Bobbie hovered over him encouragingly, and for once, drowning in her concerned gaze, Chas could think of nothing to say. Bobbie's expression turned to one of puzzlement. 'If I didn't know better I'd think you were feeling intimidated by the paper,' she said. 'But I don't think you've ever been intimidated by anything in your life.'

'Right,' said Chas trying hard for the old devil-may-care air. 'It's not the drawing, it's just the painting I'm a bit worried about.'

'Well, get started on the drawing, not too much detail, mind. The lines of the cottage and the little church in the background should come easily to you, perspective's your game, isn't it?'

If only, thought Chas, perspective was my only game.

The elation of knowing that now Mel was back, the cooking was no longer her responsibility, sent Bobbie's spirits soaring.

Added to that, the morning's demo had gone extremely well. The class appeared to have bonded for life over last evening's impromptu Italian meal and they were, on the whole, pleased with the progress they were making on the course. If it seemed that today Chas was keeping a low profile; Bobbie wasn't going to let that worry her too much. Of course not. Why should she?

Although if she admitted it, a part of her would like to stay in touch with him when the course ended tomorrow, just as a friend naturally. But if that didn't happen, well, she could live with it. In a way she'd be relieved, because non-involvement was so much easier.

Oh, he was perfectly friendly, perfectly nice; it was just that today there was an underlying seriousness about his expression that Bobbie had never noticed before.

But it was good to feel able to relax. Her last demo for the day was over; she had no more cooking responsibilities — for the foreseeable future anyway. A couple of guests had already approached her about booking next year and she'd sold two of her water colours. Roberta hummed softly to herself as she cleaned her paint brushes and pallets, which were actually three large white dinner plates.

When lunchtime came, she toyed briefly with the idea of eating with the guests as she had the previous evening. No, better not. The format she had developed of eating her meals separately meant she could get on with the stuff in the studio that needed to be done. It was surprising how much mess an art class generated.

She finished her lunch quickly in the kitchen, and took a mug of hot tea through to the studio. As a result of selling the paintings there were two gaps on the high wall where her watercolours were displayed.

From her store cupboard Bobbie took a flower study and a market scene, which she had particularly enjoyed doing.

'I'll give you a hand.' Chas had come in behind her. Bobbie felt ridiculously relieved. This morning the unwelcome thought that he was avoiding her had crossed her mind.

'Hi Chas. That's really kind.' She smiled. 'There's a ladder here and these two should fit in the gaps. My water colours are a pretty standard size.'

Chas picked up the lightweight ladder. 'You can tell me if I've hung them straight.'

'Just don't fall off the ladder. My insurance won't cover you.'

'I'm not in the habit of falling off ladders. Unlike you — I'm not accident prone.'

This is better thought Bobbie. We're back to scoring, much more comfortable. Two minutes later the pictures were in place and Chas was standing back to admire his handywork. 'I like the market scene,' he said. 'Reminds me of Sheffield a bit.'

'Gracious, I did that in the south of France, can't think of anything much less like Sheffield.'

'Well, it's mainly figures, and people don't really change country on country do they? That lady there in the blue, the one with her mouth open, now she reminds me of Marjory — can't think why.'

He started walking round examining some of the other pictures. 'I like this too,' he stopped in front of a study of a lake with hills in the background. 'Now this looks Sheffieldish — well the area round abouts anyway?'

'The Peak District, yes,' agreed Bobbie reluctantly.

'You know the Peak District? Yes, of course you do — you told me before.'

Imperceptibly Bobbie shivered. 'I know enough,' she said.

'Wonderful walks up there. The scenery's staggering.'

'So I understand.'

'The Pennines are even more spectacular. The Lake District of course, is just superb. The big lakes — you know . . . ?' Chas walked across the studio and stood with his back to her examining more of her water colours on the opposite walls. 'Your pictures are sometimes quite moody, some of them remind me of the mountains up there.'

Bobbie listened with rising panic. Any moment now he would start listing the lakes, listing the mountains. Maybe even start talking climbing accidents.

'I've got some stuff to sort out in the office,' she said in a strangled voice. 'I'll catch up with you later.'

Somehow her legs managed to support her as far as the office where she sank on to a chair. Get a grip, she told herself. The Lake District is only a place. The Great Gable is only a mountain.

Just because John died there, doesn't mean it can never be mentioned in conversation again.

'You OK?' Chas poked his head round the office door.

'Me? Yes of course I am. Why wouldn't I be?'

'You went a bit pale — I thought perhaps I'd said something to upset you.' His eyes continued to search her face.

Bobbie forced a laugh. 'I'm fine, really. I just realised the time and there's some things I have to do — that's all.'

Looking far from convinced, Chas never the less shrugged his shoulders and turned away. 'All right, I can take a hint. It was probably my boring geography lesson that did it . . . '

In the office, Bobbie tried to breathe deeply. Why was it that after all these months of keeping thoughts about John, painful memories of what had happened, what might have been, at bay; now suddenly, over the last three days, there'd been constant reminders, ever present ghosts from the past, to haunt her?

'Want another cuppa before you start?' Mel's curly dark head appeared round the door.

'No thanks, I've still got a half-finished one in the studio.'

Mel came in and sat down in front of the desk. 'I'd better get our guests accounts as up-to-date as possible. D'you think they'll be buying any more art materials?'

Bobbie shook her head. 'Shouldn't think so. Although, you know me, I'm always hopeful of maybe selling more pictures.'

Mel twisted her chair to face the computer and brought up the guest's accounts. 'Hmm. What about Chas?' she asked in a tone a little too nonchalant to be true.

Bobbie grunted, wishing she could control the faint flush she could feel spreading from her neck to her face.

'I'd say he's had a whale of a time. I'd say he was well and truly smitten.'

'Shh, keep your voice down,' whispered Bobbie. 'And he's not. Not in the least — smitten as you call it. He's just bored that's all. He was at a loose end, had to fill in time until his flat's ready and his furniture arrives. He'll have forgotten me before he turns out of the drive.'

Mel turned back to face her friend. 'And you? What about you? Will you have forgotten him, I wonder?'

Bobbie laughed. 'Nothing to forget. Oh, he's a nice enough bloke, I suppose, but you know how I feel. I'm happy with my life as it is.'

'Are you?' asked Mel softly. 'Are you

really? Look, I know it's none of my business. But this Chas seems genuine. As you said — a nice bloke. I was hoping it would be you and Lee eventually, but I can see that's not going to happen. Then along comes Chas and you're all aglow in no time . . . Don't you think you should forgive and forget John, give Chas a chance? Move on.'

Bobbie sat very straight in her chair. 'Why is it when people say: 'I know it's none of my business', they go on to presume you can't wait for their advice? You of all people should know, I have moved on.'

There was a long pause. 'And have you forgiven?'

Bobbie looked away. 'Well now, that's a bit more difficult. John lied to me. He went behind my back. In my book, that's hard to forgive . . . I know you mean well Mel, but I promise you I'm not dwelling on the past, life's too short.'

Mel sighed. 'That's OK. If you've

come to terms with it. I just hate to see you missing out on opportunities, that's all.'

Bobbie stood up. 'Got to go,' she said. 'I'll try and flog Chas one of my pictures if it makes you feel any happier. But I shouldn't hold your breath.'

# 7

The rest of the afternoon passed quickly. As promised the drizzle had disappeared and accordingly, most of the students armed with sketchbooks ventured outside to work from nature.

There were several graceful silver birches, some stately old pines and solid-looking oaks, all within a few hundred yards of the barn. Unfortunately, after about forty-five minutes the rain came down yet again so although they took it with good humour, they had to head back to the barn.

Bobbie had no more demos to do, but she spent the rest of the afternoon with her pupils, helping them to build on the confidence they'd gained on the course.

She told them that she hoped very much that, now they'd discovered that they were not the only beginners in the world, some of them would sign up for evening classes or join an art club when they arrived back in their home towns.

Now he'd got into the swing of it, Chas surprised himself at how hard he was working. He'd discovered the wet on wet technique, and the hills and trees in the background of his picture had taken on a wild and windy appearance he was secretly rather pleased with.

The house though, his architect's training wouldn't allow him to be so free with. So it nestled amongst the hills, each window as square as could be, the gable end correctly angled and every gutter and roof tile exactly executed.

'Gracious, Chas,' said Bobbie. 'You've pulled off some spectacular hills here.'

'Gosh, yes,' joined in Marjory with gusto. 'That's super, absolutely super. You've surprised yourself, haven't you? Go on admit it.'

'Please, please, spare my blushes.

One at a time now.' Chas put his brush down and stood up to stretch his legs.

'There's your tea on the tray over there,' said Bobbie. 'You looked so absorbed, I didn't like to disturb you.'

Chas looked down at her. She seemed OK now. When they'd been outside sketching the trees she'd seemed a little tense, annoyed almost. He smiled to himself. He'd thought that by moving away from his roots, he'd broken the habit of worrying about people, but it seemed as though that particular character trait would never completely disappear.

He followed Bobbie's slight figure across to the small table and helped himself to a cup of tea and two chocolate biscuits.

As they stood drinking their tea together, it dawned on Chas that if only they were alone the situation would be almost perfect.

'Are you going to have dinner with us tonight, or will you sneak off by yourself like you did at lunch time?'

There, he'd asked, and he really hadn't meant to. Only he so much wanted to see her again. And he so much needed the time to talk to her — to explain . . .

Bobbie laughed. 'I didn't sneak anywhere. It's just that I have so many things to do. And sometimes, quite frankly, I need a break.'

'OK. Point taken. I suppose that was just my clumsy way of finding out if I'd be seeing any more of you today?'

There were several dirty cups and saucers on the table. Bobbie made a great play of stacking them neatly together.

'That would be nice,' she said eventually, so softly that Chas thought he might have imagined it.

A broad beam spread across his face. 'Really?' he said. 'Well great,' he ran a hand over his hair. 'That's really great. How about after dinner? Is there another pub we can visit? Sorry, if it's a bit boring, I don't know what else to suggest. Or,' ah, a brain wave, 'how about I take you out for a meal instead?' Chas waited with baited breath.

A tide of pink flooded Bobbie's face. 'No, oh no, I couldn't possibly let you do that. I mean after last night. You . . . well, you practically cooked our meal single handedly. No, a drink would be fine. Oh, and if you like, you can pick one of my pictures — no charge of course, just a thank you. Only — if you want, of course.' She looked a little surprised at what she'd said. As though it had all spurted out of her on the spur of the moment and now she'd said it all, she wished she hadn't.

Chas put his cup on the tray and his hand on her shoulder. Suddenly he was aware that sixteen pairs of eyes were turned in their direction and the studio had become as quiet as a church.

'Sounds good,' he said, taking his hand away again. 'I'll speak to you later.'

Dinner that evening was altogether a more subdued affair. Bobbie ate her food in her flat, in front of the television, but even so she registered that there were no gales of laughter coming from the dining area.

The course was winding towards its end, which meant that after breakfast tomorrow the guests would be on their way and she would have two days freedom. She would be able to eat what she liked when she liked, be free to use the studio as she wanted, and have time to think. She was very aware that she had some thinking to do; that things had slid a little out of perspective this week, and she wasn't sure why.

Oh, she was realistic enough to recognise that Chas had had an effect on her. But whether this was the cause or the result of a subtle shift in her attitude, she wasn't so sure.

It was as though a tiny crack had occurred in the ice wall that surrounded her heart and she wasn't convinced that she could cope with the debris banked up behind it. She shrugged.

Wasn't it enough that earlier in the

afternoon, when they'd just stood there side by side sipping at their tepid tea, she'd had a moment of utter contentment and been conscious that the only thing that could possibly have made the moment better, would have been if they'd been alone? Just Chas and herself — totally alone.

Well, they would be this evening. Or they might as well be, for Roberta was planning to take Chas to another pub where, although it would be crowded, it would be quite unlikely they'd bump into anyone she knew.

They had arranged to meet at eight o'clock. Mel had offered to do all the clearing up and, when Bobbie came out of her flat door, was chatting to some of the guests who were sitting in the lounge area.

'Wow, you look nice,' commented Mel. The other guests nodded in agreement. Bobbie began to wish she'd shinned down the outside drainpipe instead of using the door.

'Thanks.' She'd only changed from

her jeans and T shirt, to a skirt and white sweater and had flung a jacket round her shoulders, but her hair shone and she'd applied eye make up and a bright lipstick instead of her usual pale lip gloss.

Chas was waiting by his car. He too had showered and changed, and looked more attractive than ever in a grey shirt and chinos. 'Hi,' he said, a little nervously. 'You look lovely. Where shall we go?'

'You drive, I'll give directions.'

The drive took them through leafy lanes, then on through the New Forest itself until they came to Lyndhurst right in the centre of the forest. After that Bobbie guessed Chas would lose track, particularly as she was giving him a potted history of the New Forest on the way.

'Did you know,' she began, 'that the word forest originally meant an area set aside for hunting to be used by the king and his powerful friends? And did you know, that the New Forest covers one hundred and forty five square miles and is the oldest forest in England? And did you know that William The Conqueror destroyed twenty-two Saxon villages in order to make it a royal hunting ground?'

'And did you know, that you are beginning to sound like my least favourite history teacher?'

'Only trying to impact a little colour and improve your knowledge,' answered Bobbie sounding a little hurt.

'I said sounded like, not looked like. Have I told you, that you look great?'

'No.'

'Well, you do. I think it's because you're smiling.'

'You make it sound as though I spend most of my time scowling.'

'Well, do you?'

'Of course I don't. Oh, you go left here.'

After a few more turns down lanes that became increasingly narrow they arrived outside a low mellow brick building that was covered with fresh green creeper and exuded warmth and charm. 'Hmm, lovely,' said Chas.

Bobbie turned towards him grinning. 'Told you I'd get you here. Good isn't it? You'd never have found it on your own. It's a bit off the beaten track. Not posh or pretentious — just really friendly and nice.'

Once inside Bobbie led the way to her favourite corner. It was cosy and intimate without being too obvious. She turned round when she heard a dull thud followed by a muffled oath.

'Ah, sorry, should have warned you about the beams,' she said trying hard not to laugh.

Rubbing his head, Chas sat down. 'I didn't know I was on some kind of sadistic trial here,' he said. 'First the impossible to follow directions, then the history test, and now you're knocking me senseless in a pub built for pygmies.'

'Sorry. Let me get you a drink.'

'Not on your life,' answered Chas. 'You'd probably end up poisoning me.'

Bobbie watched as, taking exaggerated care to avoid the low slung beams,

Chas went to the bar and came back with beer for himself and a white wine for her. For a while they talked about painting and some of the PGs and the progress they'd made. Chas, who seemed to have forgiven her for his sore head, was lavish and completely sincere with his praise.

'It's a great set up you've got,' he told her. 'You and Mel between you I mean. You deserve to do well. But you don't charge as much as I would have expected — how on earth do you make it pay?'

It was something she'd often wondered herself. The vestige of a frown appeared between her eyes. 'Well, we wanted to make sure we were always full and that word got around, so we kept our prices very competitive for the first year, but there is lots of competition in the area, so we have to stay on our toes. We've done better than expected though so far this year, so yeah, it's looking encouraging.'

'Well, I admire you,' said Chas.

'Starting a business can't be easy and you need so much capital.'

'Well Tom, Mel's fiancé, at the time — he's her husband now. He found the place. It was run down and practically derelict. It used to be a B&B, but it failed safety standards a while back so the people who ran it decided to sell. Eventually, it went to auction. There was talk of interest rates going up at the time, so there wasn't too much competition and Mel and I were lucky enough to get it.'

Chas's eyebrows nearly shot into his hair. 'Really? How on earth did you afford it? Sorry, I shouldn't have asked that. None of my business.'

'Well, we didn't buy it outright! If only. No, we've got a hefty mortgage — and some, because, we owe the builders too. Well, we owe Tom actually, because he did most of the work. We were lucky though. Well, some would say lucky. Both Mel and I were left some money. Mel's was from her godmother and mine was tied up in a trust fund until I was twenty-one, left me by my father.'

'Oh, I'm sorry,' said Chas immediately. 'I didn't realise your father was dead.'

Sympathy from Chas on this score was something she could handle. She kept her voice light. 'Oh well, it was a long time ago. I was eight, so I hardly remember him.'

'Was it an illness or something?'

Bobbie fixed her eyes on her drink. 'No, he died at the steeplechase. It's always been a dangerous sport, but he always thought luck was on his side. On that occasion his luck deserted him. He broke his back in three places.'

A hiss of breath expelled itself from between Chas's teeth. 'That must have been tough on you all.'

Bobbie turned the stem of her glass around in her fingers. 'Tough on my mum, yes. Although, she never seemed to blame him. She just got on with things because that's what you've got to do, isn't it? No good weeping and wailing and ringing your hands. She had two kids to bring up.

'Luckily we have a strong family. My grandma and granddad helped bring us up. Taught us to ride, all that kind of stuff. I had a great childhood. I was fortunate compared to some.'

She met his gaze, which looked particularly serious. 'You must have had your problems too as a kid. We've both survived so — come on, cheer up. You're on the verge of starting a whole new chapter in your life, don't look so solemn.'

I can't believe it she thought to herself. Here's me telling him not to be solemn. At the beginning of the week it was the other way round.

Chas gave a sudden grin. 'You're absolutely right,' he said. 'I've had a great few days. I've been taught how to paint like Monet, by a beautiful, talented teacher and the night is yet young . . .'

'OK. You don't have to over do it,' said Bobbie.

They didn't leave till closing time. There seemed so much to say. Chas had never seen Bobbie so relaxed or so talkative. At first he'd thought that when she'd told him about her father breaking his back at the steeplechase, the evening had to be doomed to failure. But actually when he came to think of it afterwards, she'd done most of the talking, hardly given him a chance to explain his circumstances, tell her how he felt and more importantly, that after the course finished, he wanted to see her again.

For a long moment they stared at one another, then a barmaid pointedly and noisily leaned between them to clear their glasses.

Bobbie picked up her jacket. 'I think that may be a hint.'

Chas drove back slowly; a part of him didn't want the evening to end. Bobbie had fiddled around with the radio controls and brought up some old fashioned sentimental music, which normally Chas wouldn't give the time of day. But right now it seemed to suit the mood. All too quickly they'd reached Painter's Barn. What now?

Stiffly, Chas got out of the car. By the time he'd reached the passenger door, Bobbie was already half out of her seat. He grasped for her hand.

'Thanks,' she sounded a little breathless and he could smell the scent of her hair, fell the warmth of his skin on her arm. He was still holding her hand.

'It was a lovely evening, Chas, thank you.'

He looked at her for a long moment searching for something, the right thing to say, but suddenly she smiled and reached up on tip toes to kiss the side of his cheek. Then before he could react in any way — she'd gone, leaving him listening to a song about being bewitched, bothered and bewildered.

# 8

The next morning, even though rain was once more in the air, Bobbie woke up with the beginnings of a smile on her face. The smile became broader as a feeling of well being washed through her.

Gradually shadows of the previous evening floated before her eyes. Chas grinning and rubbing his head ruefully after his encounter with the beam. Chas glancing at her sideways in the car then, saying nothing just smiling gently before returning his attention to the road. Chas standing tall and straight, looking down at her with an expression of tenderness in his eyes.

The scent of his skin, the feel of his cheek as on impulse she'd reached up and kissed it. Oh, no! She sat up in bed with her own cheeks burning. What had she been thinking about last night?

What had possessed her to make her feelings for Chas so abundantly clear?

Now she had to get through the next couple of hours, or however long it would take for Chas to get ready to leave, trying to appear normal; as though the kiss on the cheek had been nothing more than a thank you peck after a pleasant evening out. And when he'd gone, how would she manage then? Alone again, and having to carefully rebuild the fortress walls that had been guarding her heart, and for so long?

Just how had it happened? Just when did she let her guard slip that bit too far? At exactly which point did her feelings cross the line from vague liking to fierce attraction? And then simmer down from fierce attraction to . . . To what exactly?

No, no, no, best not to think about it. Let's not even go there. Bobbie got out of bed and into the shower.

When she reached the office, Mel was there before her, checking the guest's accounts.

Bobbie looked over her shoulder at the computer screen. 'Everything OK?'

'Yes, fine. Danielle's coming home today, and Amelia, of course. Pete's going to collect them. Look what I've got for her.'

Bobbie didn't like to mention that actually her enquiry had been after the accounts not Mel's new niece. 'Oh, that's so cute,' she said as Mel held up the sweetest little pink and white check dress, complete with matching knickers.

'It'll never fit you,' came a voice from the doorway.

'Oh, hi Chas,' said Bobbie with what she considered to be amazingly cool.

At the touch of a button, Mel closed down the accounts. 'Morning, Chas. Nice time last night?' She looked at her watch. 'No, don't answer that. It can't be that time already? Got to go — stuff to do in the kitchen. I'll have your bill ready after breakfast.'

'Right,' said Chas whose gaze was fixed on Bobbie.

Bobbie pushed her hair back. 'Um, I've got a lot to do too, actually.'

'I need to talk to you,' said Chas, who seemed ill at ease. 'After breakfast, if you like, but before I go.'

The large but invisible smile, that had been lighting up her insides, died an instantaneous death. He regretted last night, she could tell. Any moment now he'd start on the 'thanks, but no thanks,' speech.

And what was she thinking *LAST NIGHT* in capital letters for? It was just a drink. Just a kiss on the cheek. And thank goodness for that. At least that would make it easier to say goodbye, to pretend it had just been a fun few days.

'I'm not planning on going any-where,' she said with what she hoped was only a moderately friendly smile.

'Good,' said Chas. 'If you don't want paying till after breakfast I'll go and pack.' He turned away, then back towards her as though he wanted to say something else. 'I'll see you later then — OK?'

132

'OK.'

Trying not to feel as though her emotions were part of a big dipper, Bobbie joined Mel in the kitchen. 'We're not really running late, are we?' she asked fitting two slices of bread into the toaster.

Mel straightened up from examining the contents of the bottom shelf of the fridge. 'I was trying to be tactful.'

'Tactful? Oh, you mean Chas and me. Well, there was no need.'

Mel shot her a sidelong glance. 'Really? Just good friends still?'

'Absolutely.'

Both Mel's eyebrows shot up into her curly fringe. 'Not going to see one another again then?'

Bobbie poured herself a coffee. 'It appears not,' she said carefully — then added. 'I told you so.'

Mel slit the bacon packet open. 'Not the vibes I was picking up. I'd have said . . . '

'Look Mel, I really don't want to know — all right . . . And how much longer is this toaster going to take — that's what I would like to know.'

Mel raised her eyebrows again but wisely said nothing.

The toaster obligingly delivered the two pieces of toast with a pop. Smiling grimly, Bobbie took great pains in buttering them and applying marmalade. 'I'm having my breakfast in the studio,' she said over her shoulder. 'I've got some stuff to do.'

She regretted that kiss, Chas could tell she did. Well, maybe that would make it easier in a way to say what he had to say; to let her know that she was under a misapprehension, and that he hadn't meant for things to go this far.

He stuffed last night's shirt into the plastic bag with the rest of his washing. And what did he mean anyway, by this far? A kiss on the cheek was hardly a big deal — now was it?

The kiss had been sisterly — almost aunt-like. Nothing wrong there. It wasn't as though he'd seduced her; he's just been friendly. They were good friends, that was all. And if — just if, mind — maybe he'd thought he'd like it to go farther than that; entertained crazy romantic notions bordering on the mad passionate falling in love variety, well — he'd managed to put a curb on it — hadn't he? Yes, everything was fine, of course it was. He just had a very tiny piece of explaining to do.

The zipper on his holdall was being particularly awkward today. Chas swore softly as he wrestled with it. Would it be possible that she might still want to see him again after he'd told her what he had to tell her?

Chas sat down on the bed and put his head in his hands. For once in his life he didn't know what to do.

Breakfast was up to its usual excellent standard. Chas knew it was, not because he'd tasted or even noticed what he'd eaten, but because the other PGs told him so.

'How on earth you manage to get the bacon so exactly right, not too crispy, not too soft I'll never know,' hooted

Marjory from the end of the table. 'Geoffrey loves it, don't you, Geoffrey? He'll be sending me back here for cooking lessons next time, won't you, Geoffrey?'

After breakfast, Mel and Bobbie sat at the large dining-table and handed out the computer printed bills. Most people paid straight away, handed in their keys and departed swearing to return next year or even before. Although Chas considered Bobbie to be a little jumpy this morning, she was kind and courteous to all of them, assuring them that she'd enjoyed the course as much as they all had, and wishing them safe journeys.

Chas waited until he judged everyone else to have gone, then picked up his dirty laundry and his holdall and took them out to his car boot. He looked at the threatening sky, wondering if it were an omen.

There was only one other car left in the gravelled area where the PGs parked. He couldn't remember for sure, but he thought it belonged to the vicar. He banged his car boot shut and went in to pay his bill and make his farewells.

'You said something about me choosing one of your paintings,' he said to Bobbie, after he'd settled up and said goodbye to Mel.

'Yes, of course, come through.'

Once in the studio, Chas took his time in selecting a painting.

'Look, you don't have to have one,' said a Bobbie who looked increasingly uncomfortable.

'It's not obligatory, you know — just because I offered.'

'No, I'd love a painting. I'm just having trouble choosing. They're all so good.'

'Well, they're not, but it's nice of you to say so.'

'I'll settle for this one,' he said indicating the market scene he'd helped to hang yesterday. 'Open mouth or not, I've grown quite fond of Marjory really.'

He fetched the ladder and was soon handing the picture down to Bobbie.

'I'll wrap it for you, it won't take a moment.'

Deftly, she placed the picture on her work table and folded three sheets of tissue round it. Nervously, Chas watched.

'I'll put it behind the front seat,' he said. 'It'll be safe there.'

They both went to pick up the picture at the same time. His hands brushed against hers and they both started as though a bolt of electricity had struck. Bobbie's eyes flew to his face and Chas gave a groan and pulled her towards him.

I shouldn't be doing this, he thought, and then he stopped thinking about anything very much, except for her lips burning with his kiss, her soft arms creeping slowly round his neck and her yielding body which was melting against his.

There was the sound of knocking on the window separating the studio from the corridor, and they both swung round to find themselves staring guiltily into Marjory's interested gaze. Bobbie disentangled herself from his embrace and pushed her hair back.

Marjory opened the studio door. 'Sorry, just saying goodbye,' she hooted. 'Didn't mean to disturb anything.'

'You weren't,' said Bobbie blushing furiously.

'No, really, I was just going myself,' said Chas hurriedly leading the way out to the car park.

'It's all right, Bobbie, don't be embarrassed,' whispered Marjory just loudly enough for Chas to hear. 'I could see it coming right from the start. I said to Geoffrey, 'there's a couple if ever I saw one', and he agreed with me.'

'Really,' answered Bobbie faintly, following Chas's broad back outside to the car park where the vicar was patiently waiting.

After another round of profuse thanks, the vicar's car finally disappeared down the driveway and Chas and Bobbie were left facing one another. Chas gave a laugh that sounded strained even to his own ears. 'What was I saying about growing quite fond of Marjory, again? Her timing's good, isn't it?'

Bobbie said nothing.

'Look we'd best say goodbye,' went on Chas then found himself adding: 'For now, anyway. There's something I'd like to tell you, to explain about, but now's not the time. Can I see you soon? Some time in the week?'

Searchingly, Chas looked into her eyes. Their expression was unfathomable. She looked away, seemed undecided. Then she took a deep breath.

'OK,' she said. 'Let's make it Tuesday? Eight o'clock — how about Lyndhurst — it's about half way between here and Bournemouth — well, not as the crow flies, but you know what I mean. About eight in the main Car Park in the middle of Lyndhurst.'

'Right, I'll find it — you're on. You go in now — it's cold and it's starting to rain.'

As if to prove him correct, the

heavens opened and the rain started to fall in earnest. With a hurried wave, Bobbie ran inside. Chas was just about to put the car in gear and pull away when he remembered that he'd left the market scene picture on the studio table. He'd best go back and get it. He didn't want Bobbie to think he wasn't bothered about it, she might be hurt.

Head down he ran into the lobby. His mobile phone rang. He flicked it open. It was his brother again. 'Hi,' he said.

Bobbie reached the sanctuary of the studio and sat down feeling rather shaken. Who was she kidding with all this good friends stuff? She didn't want to be his good friend, his kiss had told her that.

Mel was right — she was in very grave danger of falling in love with him. Not just a mild flirtation, or even a casual, let's have fun affair. This was serious stuff, and she had no idea how to handle it.

This morning should have given her an inkling. When she near on panicked

141

at the thought of him driving away without taking her number or giving any indication that he wanted to see her again. But he hadn't, and he did. And he was going to see her again on Tuesday. And just how she was going to get through till Tuesday, she didn't know.

Her eyes swept round the studio and picked up the space where the market scene had been, then went on to her worktable. Oh no, he'd forgotten to take the picture.

She snatched it up and hared out of the studio. She could see through the window that his car was still there, she should be able to catch him. But when she reached the half open door to the lobby she could hear his voice, his back was towards her and obviously, he was making a phone call. Uncertainly she hovered outside the door.

' . . . bit of a chip on the shoulder, but seems to be functioning OK,' he was saying. 'Don't really think there's anything serious to worry about . . . '

There was a long pause. Then, 'Sheer stubbornness I should say — that's all. Nope, recovery's pretty complete I reckon. Yep, will do. Bye.'

Bobbie pushed the door open wider. 'Chas?'

Chas swung round as though he'd been shot.

'Sorry, did I make you jump? It's just — you left this.' She held out the picture.

'Oh, right,' he gave a relieved smile. 'Great minds think alike, I was just coming back for it. Thanks.'

They stood looking at one another, neither of them seeming able to make a move. Eventually Chas moved towards her and gave her a rather awkward hug. 'Got to go,' he said. 'See you Tuesday. Eight o'clock, main car park in Lyndhurst, right?'

Slowly, Bobbie made her way back to the kitchen. Mel was making a list of the stores she needed to replenish in order to be ready for the next guests' arrival.

'What's up?' she said on reading Bobbie's puzzled expression.

'Don't know,' said Bobbie. 'Something's not quite right.'

'I tell you what's not right. It's not right that you let that guy go walking out of here without making at least some effort to try to see him again. He's so obviously nuts about you.'

'Thank you for your thoughts on the matter Chairman Mel, but actually, I am going to see him again.'

With a delighted squeal Mel threw her arms round Bobbie's neck. 'I'm so pleased,' she said. 'You're just so right for each other. I knew it, right away. I just knew it.'

Laughing, Bobbie shook her off. 'Honestly between you and Marjory, it's a wonder he didn't make his escape long ago. Are you sure you weren't plotting together?'

'Come on tell Auntie Mel all about it. When are you going to see him again?'

Bobbie grinned. 'Tuesday. I'm meeting him in Lyndhurst.'

Mel looked doubtful. 'Well, I suppose it's a start.'

'Just a get to know you better date, that's all. Nothing too heavy. I don't know that much about him really, other than that he comes from Sheffield way, he's an architect and about to start a job in Bournemouth. It's not as though we had that much time to talk. I know his mum had arthritis and that she died a couple of years ago. I know his dad's still alive and has a new woman in his life, but I don't know anything about his friends or his hobbies — nothing like that.'

'Who cares?' asked Mel. 'The thing is you're going to see him again, the thing is you want to see him again.' She gave a sudden grin. 'It's great — isn't it?'

'Hmm,' answered Bobbie, all the time thinking to herself — there's something wrong — I know there's something wrong.

# 9

Once in the studio, Bobbie sat at her work table and allowed herself to think about what it was that was troubling her. After a slightly uncomfortable start this morning, there'd been the kiss — and it had been an amazing kiss — Bobbie admitted to herself.

Neither of them had been prepared for it, and the passion it had unleashed, she was sure, had taken them both by surprise. Chas had looked as shocked as she felt; panic stricken almost, but surely — not in a bad way. And even though they'd been interrupted, everything after that had been fine until she'd gone into the lobby and Chas had swung round to face her looking — guilty.

No, she must be wrong. What would he have to be guilty about? Was he phoning another woman? Bobbie dismissed the idea immediately — she'd had the distinct impression of a man's voice from the buzz coming from Chas's mobile.

It wasn't as though she'd caught him murmuring sweet nothings; he'd been having a normal conversation about someone to someone else who sounded like a man. Nothing wrong with that, surely. So why the guilty expression?

Thoughtfully, Bobbie stirred her coffee. Unless, of course, she'd caught him speaking about herself. For a moment she smiled at the sheer stupidity of the thought. Why would he be speaking about her to anyone? Never the less she cast her mind back, trying to recall exactly what he'd said. Something about 'functioning OK, chip on the (or was it her?) shoulder', then 'being stubborn, but nothing to worry about'.

How could any of the overheard conversation apply to her?

It was still raining outside and the air in the studio felt chilly with only her body to warm it up. She wrapped her hands round her mug. Then Bobbie's eyes widened, and darkened with fury as she realised that all of it could apply to her if someone knew her full circumstances — knew about John. Unsteadily, she placed her mug back on the work table. If, someone knew or rather, had known John. If, someone had come here to Painter's Barn deliberately, to spy on her. With shaking hands Bobbie dabbed at the coffee she'd just spilled, as the realisation hit her.

If that someone was in fact not Chas, but Spike.

Spike White — was that his name? She struggled to remember the full name of John's friend and climbing buddy. The more she thought about it the more the name *White* rang a bell.

'The pig,' she said out loud. 'Pig to end all pigs.'

Spike, was obviously a nickname. Now she came to think of it, Chas's hair was inclined to be spiky. Trying to keep cool, but burning with anger inside, Bobbie strode from the studio through the lounge area, past the big old dining table, through to the door marked *Office*.

'You still here, Mel?' she called as she passed the kitchen.

There was no reply. Grimly, Bobbie went into the office, turned on the computer and scrolled through the list of PGs. There he was. Charles White. There was his new Bournemouth address and a mobile phone number, then his car number. Under *reasons for coming on the course*, Mel had entered: *said he'd like to try something new*.

Bobbie narrowed her eyes, what was it Spike had put in the first letter she'd received from him? Something about them both being close to John and they had some talking to do, he was sure that was what John would have wanted. And what had she written back? Words to the effect that although yes, they'd both been close to John that was probably all they had in common especially as he was also a climber.

That she just wanted to get on with her life and preferred not to keep mauling over old bones, so she would rather not meet him — thank you very much.

That was more or less it — in a nutshell. And since then he'd done nothing but harass her. Well, maybe not harass, but he'd written at least twice more, so because she considered that she'd made herself clear — she'd just ignored the letters.

So now this. He'd wangled his way in here under false pretences and gradually worn down her defences. He was probably heading off to climb a mountain at this very moment.

No wonder he'd looked so uncomfortable this morning — when he realised she might have overheard his conversation. Did he really think that she would ever in her wildest dreams even consider, for one tiny second, letting a mountaineer into her life again?

And she'd never suspected. Never considered that it was all an act. Chas had made her care for him, just in order to satisfy himself that she was OK, that she was over John, so he didn't need to feel guilty anymore. For a moment Bobbie blinked back angry tears. She'd fallen for it hook line and sinker.

Full of fury, Bobbie stared at the screen in front of her, trying hard to forget the expression in his eyes as he smiled down at her, the feel of his hand on her back, the way their conversation had flowed so easily and — the kiss.

When they'd gone out on the first evening, he'd been so nice, so understanding when she'd said she wasn't in the market for a relationship. Well of course he would be, wouldn't he?

He didn't need to ask the obvious question of — why not? He knew already.

And when he'd found the picture, her picture of John, he'd commented on the sensitivity of the drawing. A comment guaranteed to make her feel that he was the most understanding man on earth. Huh. He was nothing but a cheap con-man.

Bobbie was so furious, she generated a new wave of energy and cleaned the studio in record time, checked her supplies of paints and paper ready for the next course and let the cleaners in. Then she got into her car and drove.

At first she drove in no particular direction just towards the sea. Then she decided she needed some fresh air and, as the rain had petered out now and the sky was looking a little brighter, she parked in the big Municipal car park on the top of the cliffs at Barton on Sea.

With no hesitation she took the cliff path towards Highcliff Castle and gardens. It was a walk she'd taken many times before. She loved the view of the clean fresh sea and the sound it made as it beat and sucked the pebbles along the shore line. The sound had often acted as a salve on her battered emotions in the past.

So what was she going to do about

Chas? What would she say to him when she met him? Because she was going to keep their date, of that she was determined.

Should she act love struck, gaze deeply into his eyes, hang on to his every word? Say — 'oh, Chas you are so wonderful'? No, Bobbie knew she wouldn't be able to pull that off.

Bobbie dashed the back of her hand across her eyes. Only she was, wasn't she, completely stupid? And now completely miserable as well. She was very glad there were only a few seagulls around to witness her total humiliation as she gave in and cried angry, heartbroken tears until she reached Highcliff.

\* \* \*

Once at Highcliff she wandered up the cliff path and through the gardens. At first she didn't notice the rain in the air then, all at once she was in the middle of another April shower, only this was more of a deluge. Dripping wet, she ducked into the tea room in the grounds of Highcliff Castle.

Once inside, she shook the rain off her face and took off her soaking jacket.

'Well, well, what on earth are you doing here?'

Bobbie pushed her damp hair back and made out, through a mist of tears that were thankfully now mixed with rain, Lee grinning all over his face. He was sitting together with a very pretty blonde, who although Bobbie couldn't immediately put a name to her, looked familiar.

'Hello,' said Bobbie pulling herself together fast and trying to sound happy and carefree. 'I've been cooped up in the studio for three days, I needed a bit of air.'

'Come and sit down,' Lee dragged over another chair. He put an arm over the blonde girl's shoulders. 'This is Kirsty, she sometimes helps out in the shop.'

'Oh yes, of course. I thought I

recognised you — how're you doing?'

Kirsty smiled which made her look even prettier. 'I've just eaten a huge piece of chocolate gateau and you ask me that?'

Lee pulled up a chair and Bobbie sat down with her, more than welcome, cup of tea. 'Unusual for you,' she said to Lee. 'Out here at this time of the day.'

Lee looked at his watch. 'Well, loosely speaking, this is our lunch hour. We tend to eat away from the shop, for obvious reasons, but at least when you're the boss you can choose your lunch time.'

Obvious reasons. So Bobbie had been right when she'd picked up the feeling that the two of them were a couple.

'We've got another ten minutes,' said Kirsty. 'D'you want another coffee, Lee?'

'No thanks,' said Lee looking at her adoringly, 'but you have one to wash down the gateau.'

Kirsty went over to the counter.

Bobbie took a sip of scalding tea. 'You were looking very cosy when I came in.'

Lee flushed, then gave a rueful grin. 'Not much gets past you, does it? Truth is, I've known Kirsty a while and well, it didn't look as though I was ever going to get anywhere with you, especially since this Chas bloke arrived on the scene.' He shot her a penetrating glance. 'I rather thought you had something going there? Seems a nice enough guy.'

Bobbie concentrated hard on lifting her cup from the saucer. 'You know me Lee. Chas and I are just good friends, I'm still not in the market for a relationship.'

Kirsty was on her way back to the table. 'Not the signals I was picking up but, if you say so. You should give it a whirl though. You're missing a lot of fun,' he added as Kirsty sat down.

Trying not to feel like an outsized

gooseberry, Bobbie drank the rest of her tea as quickly as she could without burning her mouth. And as soon as the rain became no more than a fine drizzle and the sun came out, accepted a lift back to Barton on Sea to pick up her car.

She sat in the back of Lee's car listening to Kirsty and Lee having a conversation about the shop, and watched the way they glanced at one another smiling when there really wasn't anything obvious to smile about. Suddenly, she felt very lonely.

Bobbie didn't know how she got through the next few days. The new intake of PGs were somehow nothing like as interesting as the last crowd had been.

Although Chas had rung twice, once leaving a message on the answer phone that he hoped she'd call him back (she hadn't) and once speaking to Mel because Bobbie was thankfully tied up with a demonstration workshop, the thought of his persistence didn't redeem him in her eyes.

'I don't understand you, Bobbie,' said Mel on delivering Chas's message. 'The poor guy clearly wants to speak to you so why don't you put him out of his misery?'

'He knows I'm meeting him on Tuesday,' replied Bobbie logically. 'There's nothing else to say.'

Mel shrugged her shoulders. 'Has anyone ever told you how stubborn you can be?'

'Yep,' answered Bobbie. 'Quite recently as it happens.'

★　★　★

It was Tuesday at last. Chas was vaguely disturbed that Bobbie hadn't returned his calls. Still, he'd seen at first hand how occupied her days were, she'd probably not had much time, and maybe she'd been a little nervous, after that kiss, about what she would say. He let his mind linger a little on that kiss. Yes, it was probably best under the circumstances that she hadn't rung.

Truth to tell, he'd felt uneasy himself since that kiss, not that he'd done anything wrong exactly, by not telling her the whole truth. In fact he felt he'd been very circumspect under the circumstances, treated Bobbie and her feelings with cautious solicitude.

He caught himself up, who was he kidding, he'd known how attracted he was to Bobbie right from the start. He should have made his position clear immediately.

Yes, but then she might not have given him the time of day — and he would never have stood a chance.

Just as well, he hadn't had much time to brood over the situation. He'd picked up the keys to his new flat and spent some time altering his bedroom from baby pink to calico.

After that he'd changed the particular nasty-looking carpet in his sitting-room to wooden flooring, which didn't go down quite as easily as the manufacturers had led him to believe it would.

However, once finished, Chas stood back, surveyed his work and allowed himself to be satisfied with the results.

He found he was trying to see the flat through Bobbie's eyes and even went so far as to bring round the friends he'd been staying with, for their opinion, being rather more interested in Debbie's ideas on the subject than Andy's.

So now it was Tuesday and at eight o'clock he was meeting Bobbie in Lyndhurst. His furniture was being delivered from storage on Thursday, and who knew, he might even be entertaining Bobbie at his new pad in Bournemouth at the weekend. His stomach lurched at the very thought.

He hoped he would be able to find the car park in Lyndhurst where he was to meet Bobbie. He knew it was the main car park, and that it was off the main drag. Everyone he'd spoken to said he couldn't miss it. In the end, because he'd also been told the traffic could be unpredictable, and he didn't want to be late, Chas reached there long before eight.

Feeling ridiculously jumpy, he found a space positioned so that he'd be able to spot her car as she drove in. After five minutes of fidgeting with the controls on his radio, and nervously smoothing down a spike of hair that insisted on standing in the wrong direction, he got out of the car in order to stretch his legs.

A few minutes later, after receiving a suspicious glance from a passing librarian, or what Chas imagined a librarian to look like, he got in again quickly in case he was arrested for loitering with intent.

Ah, here she was.

Chas's heart did a complete somersault and then a crash landing against his ribs. It left him slightly short of breath. She hadn't seen him yet. He kept still and watched as Bobbie deftly backed into a space, only then did she cast her eyes round the half empty car park and eventually recognise his car.

The smile on his lips died. He knew immediately that there was something very, very, wrong.

# 10

Now she was here Bobbie found she was shaking. The shakes had started just as soon as she'd spotted him swinging his legs out of the car, the same lopsided grin on his face, the same twinkle in his eyes.

She took a deep breath, smoothed a hand over her already smooth hair and fixed a bright smile on her face.

'You found it then?' Obvious question, but it would do to start the ball rolling.

'Hello Chas, how are you?' answered Chas.

'I was going to say that next,' said Bobbie grinning. Whoa, this was not the way to start. Don't get too friendly. Don't let the magic start working. Just remember, he's a fraud. He's the enemy. 'So, how're things?'

'Things are good. Well, the flat's

habitable now. I'm just waiting for my furniture.'

They walked along, side by side, Bobbie taking great care to keep her bag on the inside arm so he couldn't take her hand, she wasn't sure how she would respond if he were to touch her.

'Well, where shall we go? Have you eaten?'

'No, but I thought we'd take a walk first.'

'Suits me.'

'I could show you, for example, the parish church, which is Victorian gothic in style, and had ornamentation by Millais, who was English, not to be confused with Millet, who was French.'

'Can we stop the history of art lessons now teacher?'

'I could also show you, in the churchyard, the grave of Alice Liddell, the original Alice in *Alice In Wonderland*.'

'Is that a fact?'

'Yes. I was never a fan of Alice in Wonderland myself. Too confusing, I'm a simple girl at heart. Can't stand it if I find I've been lied to.'

Chas took a sidelong glance at her, opened his mouth, then shut it again.

They were walking quite quickly now; Bobbie realised; so if Chas had expected a leisurely saunter he must be feeling surprised. Good, she wanted to keep him guessing. Although, come to think of it she also wanted to be able to watch his expression when she really tore into him, and walking at fast pace — that would be a no, no.

'Would you mind if I changed my mind?' she asked with a brilliant smile.

Chas looked confused. Even better.

'About eating, I mean. Actually, I think a drink and a packet of crisps would be a great idea.'

'Fine, absolutely fine,' agreed Chas, breathing more easily.

The next pub they came to looked inviting, but not yet, too busy. Chas ordered the drinks while Bobbie found a secluded corner.

'Well, this is nice,' said Chas placing

her drink in front of her then taking a chair opposite.

'Yes, isn't it?' agreed Bobbie in icily polite tones.

Chas gave an exasperated sigh. 'Look, what exactly is the matter with you?'

Bobbie widened her eyes in mock surprise. 'Nothing wrong with me Chas, I've got nothing to hide.'

'What's that meant to mean?'

Narrowing her eyes, she looked straight at him. 'Well, what d'you think it means, Chas? Or should I say Spike?' There, she'd got him, right in the solar plexus.

He looked dumbfounded and a slow blush washed over him. Then he laughed. 'You think I'm Spike?'

Wait a minute, this wasn't going quite according to plan. 'Oh, stop acting, for goodness sake. I know you're Spike, so there's no point pretending.'

'And how exactly, did you figure that out?'

For a long moment Bobbie met his

eyes, they looked surprisingly honest for a multiple deceiver.

'Well, you are, you must be,' she started, feeling less confident by the second. 'Otherwise, how do you know so much about me? How did you know about John? And don't tell me — lucky guess, or that you didn't know — because I can see from your face that you did.'

Chas took a leisurely drink of his beer glass. 'We have to get a few things straight,' he said when he'd carefully placed his glass back on the beer mat in front of him. 'First yes, I did know about you and John. I knew because my middle brother is Spike. Yes, that's right. Not me, my brother. I only met John once — nice guy. I liked him . . .

'Now, when John died, my brother wasn't with him. John had gone on the climb last minute, to fill in. After the accident my brother was devastated, and I don't exaggerate. He was even more devastated when you didn't come to the funeral, and you wouldn't answer his letters.'

Bobbie felt the colour drain from her face. 'I couldn't . . . ' she started.

'I know you never had much time for climbing,' went on Chas, after a moment spent scrutinising her face. 'As it happens I haven't either. But they had this code. If someone meets with an accident, their climbing buddy rallies round, tries to help the other one's girl . . . You might not realise just how seriously my brother took your total rejection of his help.'

Not taking her eyes off her drink, Bobbie sat motionless. In a moment he'll stop, she thought.

In a moment I'll get my thoughts together and this terrible pain in my chest will go away.

'Now me,' Chas went on. 'I advised him to forget it. I said that people grieve in their own way and if you wanted no contact, to leave it. He, on the other hand, is probably more sensitive than I am, middle children usually are, so I understand. Spike thought you were in denial. He thought you might be letting it ruin your life. He thought you needed to talk — that you had unfinished business . . . So have you? Got unfinished business?'

'Just don't — don't mention the word 'closure'. If I hear that word one more time I'll throw up.' Ah, that was better, Bobbie was feeling angry again. Anger was a much easier emotion to handle than grief. 'So OK, you're not Spike, but just because you're his brother, what right does that give you to come sneaking around here spying on me?'

Chas looked away, over to the bar, which was filling up rapidly. 'Look, I was in the area. My brother wrote to you to explain that I might call in. OK, so I was wrong, when I realised you'd either never got the letter or had destroyed it unread, I was wrong not to explain right away. But well, I liked you. I decided to join the course so I could get a better idea of how you were doing.

I thought you looked sad, and I could see Spike might be right, you might be letting it ruin your life.'

Bobbie nearly snorted. 'Oh please! I'm running a successful business here, do I look as though my life is ruined?'

Chas gave a smile. 'No, not from the outside, that's for sure . . . So I can tell him now, can I? I can say — don't worry about Roberta; she's doing absolutely fine. She's got it all sussed. Making a go of what she's doing — loves her work — sells her painting. Look, here's one of hers. Good, isn't it? Look at those happy, happy colours spilling out of the frame.

'Oh yes, and she still keeps one of John in her flat, sometimes it's face down — depending on her mood . . . But she never mentions him and when someone else does — her eyes go blank and she turns away . . . Oh, and she's not in the market for a new relationship, doesn't believe in love any more. Thinks it's an overrated emotion. That's right, isn't it — that's more or less what you think?'

Eyes sparkling, Bobbie looked up. 'Have you quite finished?'

Chas leaned forward. 'Actually no, I haven't. Did it ever occur to you, that my brother might also be going through hell over this? He's been beating himself up for nigh on eighteen months. You see — it should have been him who went climbing that day.

'He had no idea about John's promise to you. John took his place as a favour . . . Just imagine how that must feel?'

For a moment Bobbie felt sick. Had she really been so selfish, thinking only of herself and how she was feeling? But surely, surely she was justified.

'You don't understand. John knew how I felt about the climbing. In fact, as soon as I found out how large a part it played in his life, I told him we were over, that I couldn't handle dangerous hobbies.'

'So what happened?'

Bobbie shivered. 'We both spent a

miserable few weeks apart. Then he turned up on my doorstep with an engagement ring, swearing he'd never go climbing again.'

She heard Chas's sharp intake of breath.

'Yes, well, we both know how much that promise meant to him,' she said bitterly. 'That's why, I need to forget him. And I am, I have . . . Forgotten him — I mean.'

'Not forgiven though?'

'I'm working on it.'

Bobbie watched Chas's strong brown fingers turning a beer mat round and round on the table.

'I wonder how you'd have felt, if he'd asked you to give up painting?'

'Oh please — hardly the same thing.'

'Don't see why not.'

'People die on mountains. What am I going to do? Stab myself to death with a paint brush?'

There was a long silence. Then, from somewhere deep inside, a chuckle escaped her. She met Chas's eyes and suddenly both of them were laughing, only Bobbie's laughter abruptly turned into deep choking sobs.

'Oh no,' she sniffed between tears that she was fighting to keep silent. 'I'm so sorry. How embarrassing . . . '

Not looking in the least embarrassed, Chas handed her a handkerchief across the table and watched as she struggled to pull herself together.

'You should have gone to the funeral, let all this lot out there,' he said. 'Why didn't you?'

Bobbie bit her lip and looked out of the window with blurred vision. 'I couldn't,' she whispered. 'I wanted to, but I couldn't.'

'It would have been better if you had.'

'D'you think I don't know that? I couldn't go because I was in hospital with a burst appendix.'

Momentarily dumbfounded, Chas stared across at her. Then sympathy flooded his face. 'Oh no,' he said as though he just couldn't believe it. 'Oh

Bobbie. So all this time you've not only been broken hearted, you've been beating yourself up because you couldn't go to the funeral and you feel as though you let him down. That's it, isn't it?'

Through her tears, Bobbie nodded. 'I suppose so. Although, I never thought of it like that. I just felt so rotten, for so long. Then when I felt a little better I just wanted to put everything behind me and do what they say. Move on,' she looked up with a half smile. 'Only I discovered it's not quite as easy as all that.'

Chas reached for both her hands across the table. 'Bobbie, Bobbie, Bobbie. What am I going to do about you?'

'Have I got mascara all over my face?'

'No.'

'Why are you staring at me like that then?'

'Because Bobbie, there are a lot of things I want to say, but the timing as always, is bad. Now, do you want to eat

174

here? Go somewhere else? Or not eat at all?'

Bobbie wiped her eyes for the last time, and gave a shaky smiled. 'Oh somewhere else I think,' she said. 'Suddenly I'm starving.'

# 11

Smiling softly to herself, Bobbie put the final touch to the poppies she was painting, wet in wet style, for a friend of her mother's. She stood back to assess the effect of the dark centres against the vivid crimson of the papery petals. Yep, that would do it. No more fiddling now or she'd lose that spontaneous something that made the difference between a successful and merely acceptable piece of work.

Humming to herself a song about being addicted to love, she cleaned her paintbrushes and pallet, stretched luxuriously and glanced at her wrist watch. She wandered through to the empty kitchen. It was good to have the whole of Painter's Barn to herself for a change. No PGs for another two days. Great!

The fridge was still pretty well

stocked. She checked it again. Yes, the birthday champagne, that was now at least six months old, was chilling nicely; the pasta was there sitting on its shelf next to a bag of salad, and Mel's sauce — the bolognese only this time, was thawing out nicely.

Bobbie opened the back door and strolled down the garden intending to pick some primroses to set in a small posy vase at the centre of the small table for two laid ready in her flat. The resident blackbird was giving it what for from the top of the weather vane.

'OK, OK, I hear you,' said Bobbie. 'I know what you're saying and I've done it haven't I? My life is back on track.'

She squinted up at the blackbird and spotted a pretty, blue clematis that must have come out in the last couple of days. Now, she knew it was really summer, she thought as she picked a couple of blooms. The first flowers of that particular clematis were never out before the end of May. The sigh that escaped her lips was one of utter contentment.

It was hard to believe that two whole months had gone since the day Chas first turned up at Painter's Barn. She cast her mind back, trying hard to remember how exactly she had been feeling that day, when she'd backed through the door — arms full of artists materials — straight into his arms. She'd been scared, that's how she'd been feeling. Not scared of living so much as scared of feeling. Well, now with Chas's help, all that was behind her.

Together they'd gone to Chas's home in Sheffield. She'd met Spike, a more serious slightly nervy, edition of his older brother, but complete with lighter hair that was even spikier.

Tactfully, Chas had left them alone and after the first few awkward minutes, Bobbie had found herself telling Spike all about John, and his enthusiasm for life. About the places they'd been together and the things they'd discussed, and found, that it was as though a dam had burst inside her.

'I'm so glad you came at last,' said Spike. 'I know how much John loved you.'

Bobbie nodded, unable to speak for the tears queuing up behind her eyelids.

Later in the weekend they'd taken a trip to Wasdale Head on Wast Water which was where John's ashes had been scattered. All three of them had strolled through the small churchyard, and looked up towards the south face of the Great Gable, and England's highest mountain, the imposing Scafell Pike.

Looking at the magnificent, but treacherous and unforgiving Lakeland peaks, Bobbie had shivered. But at the same time she realised that although she'd never felt closer to John than she did while staring at the majestic landscape that he had loved so much, she was ready to forgive both herself and him for not being perfect. She was ready now to say goodbye to him.

When they'd arrived back at the New

Forest, she'd asked for a breathing space and miracle of miracles, Chas had understood.

'Just don't make it too long,' he'd said looking steadily into her eyes. 'I'm a patient man, but well, not that patient.'

So now it was the end of May, the sun was shining, the table laid and the champagne on ice. Bobbie came back in from the garden, showered and changed into a simple dress and strappy sandals.

She brushed her pale brown hair and applied a light touch of makeup, then she walked through to her small sitting-room, took her drawing of John from the wall, looked at it one more time, then slid it into a drawer.

Funnily enough, she didn't feel nervous. Excited, yes. Elated, definitely. But nervous, no, she didn't think so.

The scrunch of tyres on gravel sounded outside. Then the clang of the outside doorbell. Bobbie checked her reflection again. She thought she looked

OK, her hair was shining, her eyes sparkling with anticipation.

I'm ready, she said out loud. I've waited long enough.

Chas was lounging in the doorway, his hair very dark, with just a tiny bit on the crown sticking up in the wrong direction. His twinkly eyes were a very pale piercing blue against his lightly tanned skin, and there was a questioning smile playing about his firm mouth.

'Hi.' His eyes locked on hers. 'I understand you have a broken heart. Can I help you to unbreak it?'

Bobbie took a step towards him and melted into his arms. 'I thought you'd never ask.'

**THE END**

We do hope that you have enjoyed reading this large print book.

Did you know that all of our titles are available for purchase?

We publish a wide range of high quality large print books including:
**Romances, Mysteries, Classics**
**General Fiction**
**Non Fiction and Westerns**

Special interest titles available in large print are:
**The Little Oxford Dictionary**
**Music Book, Song Book**
**Hymn Book, Service Book**

Also available from us courtesy of Oxford University Press:
**Young Readers' Dictionary**
**(large print edition)**
**Young Readers' Thesaurus**
**(large print edition)**

For further information or a free brochure, please contact us at:
**Ulverscroft Large Print Books Ltd.,**
**The Green, Bradgate Road, Anstey,**
**Leicester, LE7 7FU, England.**
**Tel:** (00 44) **0116 236 4325**
**Fax:** (00 44) **0116 234 0205**

*Other titles in the
Linford Romance Library:*

## DARK MOON

### Catriona McCuaig

When her aunt dies, Jemima is offered a home with her stern uncle, but vows to make her own way in the world by working at a coaching inn. She falls for the handsome and fascinating Giles Morton, but he has a menacing secret that could endanger them both. When Jemima is forced to choose between her own safety and saving the man she loves, she doesn't hesitate for a moment — but will they both come out of it alive?

# HOME IS WHERE
# THE HEART IS

## Chrissie Loveday

Jayne and Dan Pearson have moved to their dream house . . . a huge dilapidated heap on top of a Cornish cliff. The stresses of city life are behind them, their children consider their new home 'the coolest house ever', and the family's future looks rosy. But when a serious accident forces them to re-think their dream, they embark upon a completely different way of life — though its pleasures and disasters bring a whole new meaning to the word *stress* . . .

# A HATFUL OF DREAMS

## Roberta Grieve

Sally Williams works in a milliner's salon, but her ambition is to own her own shop. When she delivers a hat to Lady Isabelle Lazenby, she becomes flustered by Lady Isabelle's handsome cousin, Charles Carey — but finds herself attracted to the footman, Harry. However, Charles' interest in Sally causes a rift in her friendship with Harry, who also seems to be close with Maggie, Lady Isabelle's maid. Will Sally achieve her ambition? And could there be a future for Sally and Harry?

# LOVE GAME

## Diney Delancey

Rowena Winston had enjoyed working with her dear friend Donald. Together they had turned Chalford Manor into an excellent hotel and country club. But now Donald was dead, and she had the far greater challenge of working with his younger brother Clive — a man who had every reason to resent her!